Slanting his mo
a smooth glide,
and teasing, he
hinted and lured rather than
taking outright.

Cali shuddered, her breath slipping over his lips with a soft moan. He pulled back to meet her gaze. "That good, huh?"

Her lips curved as she drank him in through half-lidded eyes. "I'd forgotten *just how good* that felt." The tip of her tongue darted out to moisten the sexy swell of her pink bottom lip.

"Wasn't much of a kiss, if you ask me," he murmured. "I can do better."

Her eyes darkened like smoked sea glass and locked on his mouth, sending "go" signals toward his groin. Her breath hitched as, moving closer, he traced the smooth line of her delicate jaw with his thumb, sifted his fingers through the silky hair at the nape of her neck, and tilted her face to his.

"Maybe just one more," she whispered breathlessly, her lips an enticing invitation.

"One more," he agreed, intent on doling out a kiss with every skill and seductive nuance he'd honed since high school packed into it. And that kiss would become the prelude to a night in bed.

Dear Reader

Have you ever had a connection to a place that neither time nor distance could sever?

I have. Chicago.

It's the city of my youthful heart and romantic memories. It's where I grew up, became a woman, and learned to love. When I began writing WILD FLING OR A WEDDING RING? I found myself mentally walking the streets, dropping by old haunts, and picking out all that I loved about the city to give to my heroine, Cali, to discover.

In the end this book became a bit of a love letter to Chicago, and I hope I'll be able to share some of what makes this city so special to me with you.

Do you have a city that's stolen your heart? If so, drop by my website at www.miralynkelly.com and share your stories.

Mira

WILD FLING OR A
WEDDING RING?

BY
MIRA LYN KELLY

MILLS & BOON®

MODERN
Heat™

First published in Great Britain 2010
Harlequin Mills & Boon Limited,
Eton House, 18-24 Paradise Road, Richmond, Surrey TW9 1SR

© Mira Lyn Sperl 2010

ISBN: 978 0 263 87738 0

Harlequin Mills & Boon policy is to use papers that are natural, renewable and recyclable products and made from wood grown in sustainable forests. The logging and manufacturing process conform to the legal environmental regulations of the country of origin.

Printed and bound in Spain
by Litografia Rosés, S.A., Barcelona

Mira Lyn Kelly grew up in the Chicago area, and earned her degree in Fine Arts from Loyola University. She met the love of her life while studying abroad in Rome, Italy, only to discover he'd been living right around the corner from her for the previous two years. Having spent her twenties working and playing in the Windy City, she's now settled with her husband in rural Minnesota, where their four beautiful children provide an excess of action, adventure and entertainment.

With writing as her passion, and inspiration striking at the most unpredictable times, Mira can always be found with a notebook at the ready. (More than once she's been caught by the neighbours, covered in grass clippings, scribbling away atop the compost container!)

When she isn't reading, writing, or running to keep up with the kids, she loves watching movies, blabbing with the girls, and cooking with her husband and friends. Check out her website www.miralynkelly.com for the latest dish!

This is Mira's first book!

To my husband, Chris. I love you.

CHAPTER ONE

STYLED in 1930s décor, the Jazz House was an inconspicuous place, classy and understated, tucked into a quiet corner of Chicago's downtown Streeterville neighborhood. Smoky melodies, thick with heartbreak and yearning, drifted through the dark club, curling around hushed conversations and seeping beneath the tensions of the day.

Seated toward the back of the high-polish bar, Calista McGovern swirled rough chunks of ice in her gin and tonic, savoring the pull of blue notes at her soul. This was a place she could get used to.

That was it would be, if the next two months weren't committed to an assignment that left little chance of Cali seeing the light of day—or even the dark of night for that matter—before it ended. She was Project Manager for the multibillion-dollar retail conglomerate MetroTrek, and her stint in the Windy City guaranteed long hours under the steady hum of fluorescent lights, broken only by meals on the run and the necessity to sleep.

Chicago was about work. It was a stepping stone to the new London expansion position her New York-based boss, Amanda Martin, had all but promised her—if she could nail the Chicago job first. It was the opportunity Cali had been waiting for.

Her plane had touched down on the O'Hare tarmac three

hours before. She would have been elbow-deep in work already if it hadn't been for Amanda's insistence that she spend her first night in Chicago out on the town. And, more specifically, at this club.

As a rule, Cali wasn't much of a suck-up, but with the London position hovering on the horizon—the restoration of a career she'd nearly destroyed all but complete—catering to her boss's whims seemed a reasonable accommodation.

Amanda had discovered the club through her little sister's husband, Jackson, last time she'd been home for a visit, and hadn't stopped talking about it since. Normally mention of anything associated with the beloved brother-in-law earned a mental eye-roll from Cali. As Amanda told it—often in excruciating detail—Jackson could do no wrong. As Cali heard it, Amanda harbored some deep-seated crush on the guy, and any opinion even remotely tied to him should be taken with a grain of salt.

Tonight, however, Cali had to give the man credit. The Jazz House was perfect, with precisely the kind of subdued atmosphere she appreciated. Or at least it was until a guy looking to be in his mid-forties pushed onto an empty stool beside her and let out a labored breath as he rubbed a bloodshot eye with the back of his thumb.

"Don't I know you from somewhere?"

Jake Tyler rested one shoulder against the wall, his attention locked on the woman at the bar. From the minute he'd seen her shake that spill of sexy red-brown curls across her shoulders he'd been struck immobile. He'd watched her face relax and her lips curve as she listened to the music, enjoyed the way her skirt rode over her thigh as she crossed her long, smooth legs, and wondered what it would be like to touch her. Take her home and lose himself in her body.

But picking up company wasn't part of the plan. He'd come to unwind, as he often did after too many hours in the operating room. To let the smooth jazz ease the strain in his muscles and his mind before heading home to get some much needed sleep.

So he'd tried to focus on the music instead of the pretty girl at the bar, and he'd done an almost passable job of it—right up to when the chump running on one drink too many moved in.

Now the woman with the siren hair and soft smile was unsuccessfully trying to brush off the persistent nuisance who wanted to play the "don't I know you from somewhere" game.

It was a cheap line, so overdone it should be stricken from the pick-up playbook forever. But some guys never learned. And some women deserved a break. Which was why, when the guy moved in again, Jake pushed off the wall and crossed to the bar.

A thick cloud of cologne, laced with sweat and whiskey, wafted around her as the man hunched closer. Cali set her glass down and reached for her purse.

This stank. The music was fantastic, but she couldn't shake her barfly, which meant it was time to leave.

"You're alone." The slurred voice dropped meaningfully. *"I'm* alone—"

"Hey, babe." A rich, deep baritone cut in, sliding like a smooth caress down her spine, saving her from whatever promise or threat of mutual satisfaction Whiskey Breath was selling. The body that issued it dropped into the open seat on her left, and when his warm, wide hand settled over hers she jumped, awareness churning within her. "Hope I didn't keep you waiting too long. Work ran late."

"What—?" was all she managed, before her first look at the stranger beside her stole her breath. Piercing blue eyes pinned her to her spot, while a smile as sexy as sin held her rapt.

Dangerous.

Next to this guy, Mr. Whiskey was nothing. She should push away from the bar, grab her clutch and leave without looking back.

That was what she should do.

Definitely.

Sensual lips, full and wide, cocked up to one side, and before she'd even thought, the words left her lips. "Hi…babe."

Her gaze dragged over the near-hypnotic proportions of her barside savior, as he followed the other man's grudging retreat with his eyes. He was huge, easily six-four, built with a tapered physique that left her mouth watering and the rest of her body on high alert. The thin black knit of his summer-weight V-neck clung, emphasizing his broad shoulders, defined pecs and flat abs. This was the kind of man she never let her herself notice, only this one….

Well, he was a modern-day knight in pricey denim, rescuing a damsel in distress from a whiskey-breathing barfly. He was her hero and, try as she might not to notice, she wasn't dead.

He shot her a disarming smile. "Sorry about the 'babe' business, but it had the necessary possessive ring to it, don't you think?"

He had an incredible voice.

Fighting the urge to titter with nervous laughter, she answered, "Very effective. Thank you." She cleared her throat, wishing her head would clear as well. She was a grown woman, and this wasn't the first attractive man who'd ever spoken to her—though he was easily the most attractive. The lean, chiseled lines of his cheekbones and the ruthless cut of his jaw and nose were masculine, sexy. Blending outdoor sportsman and tuxedo-fine in seamless perfection. The thick silk of his dark hair, clipped short on the sides and long enough to wave in rumpled disarray on top, had her fingers itching to tangle in it.

Definitely dangerous.

He angled closer, an alluring violation of her personal space, and offered his hand with a gruff introduction. "Jake Tyler."

"Cali—but, umm, I should get going."

He turned to face her, those blue eyes filled with censure. "After I got rid of your friend? The least you can do to thank me is stay and listen to the music, like you were trying to do before he interrupted."

So he'd been watching her. Boy, she didn't want to know that. Didn't want to like it. Slanting a look his way, she tried to size up the threat he made.

He met her stare and held it for a beat. "You seemed to be enjoying the band." He shrugged and glanced over to where the bartender had set down his order.

The long muscles running the length of his spine, visible through the hug of his sweater, flexed and shifted as he rested one arm on the bar to reach for his drink.

"I like jazz. I like it when others like it, too. The guy seemed to be getting in the way, so I helped him out. That's all. You and I, we can just sit here and listen together. Ignore each other completely. In fact…" he leaned back slightly, eyes focused now on the front of the club "…I've forgotten about you already."

She stared, and then a ripple of amusement broke loose from the anxiety-tightened confines of her chest. His reverse psychology teasing should have sent her fleeing for the nearest cab, only it had sent butterflies flitting around her belly instead.

Temptingly dangerous.

She cocked her brow at him, feigning surprise. "Are you still here?"

The low rumble of his answering laughter had a seductive quality she couldn't resist, and then she was laughing too, swearing to herself it was only a momentary indulgence.

"Fine," he drawled, luring her attention to the mischievous gleam in his eyes. "Since you're so desperately chatty, I'll talk to you."

A stuttering cough escaped her as she tried to muster any emotion other than delight. "I beg your pardon?"

The corner of his mouth turned up. "No need to beg. So, what do you think? Should we talk about work?"

He was good. Smooth. Exactly the kind of distraction she didn't need on the first day of the most important assignment since the reinvention of her career. She didn't have room in her life for a man. She should run, she thought, firmly planted in her spot.

But, she'd run every other time a man threw a decent line or a flashy smile her way over the last three years. She'd tolerated no distractions and it had worked. She'd gotten herself where she wanted to go.

Only tonight she didn't want to run.

Maybe it was the music, or the club, or the high she was riding being so close to her goal. Or maybe she just wanted to remember what it felt like to have a gorgeous man trying for her smile. After all, it wasn't as though this Jake Tyler was asking her to dump her career to be with him. He was just a sexy bit of sporting flirtation. Harmless. Fun. A guy she'd never see again and couldn't affect her future one iota.

But talking about work? No way. Work was all tied up, with her every hope, dream and ambition wrapped around it—and her biggest mistake behind it.

No. Her career was just for her. Much too intimate for sharing with a sporting flirtation.

Cali took a sip of her drink. Brushed at the drops of condensation with her thumb. "Let's skip work. I'll be up to my ears in it for the next few months. This is the last night of calm before I lose my life and identity to the job completely."

"Ah, you're a spy, then," he offered, with an understanding nod and a devastating grin. "Me too."

Two hours later Jake sat back, enjoying the full-bodied, free sound of Cali's laughter as her head tilted back, her eyes closed. It was a sound as enticing as any he'd ever heard, and he'd been working all evening to earn more of it. Now, as her laughter eased into a sigh, her smile became hesitant. She pushed a loose curl behind her ear and turned to him.

Damn, she was gorgeous.

He wanted her. And, with the way her heavy-lidded stare kept slipping to his mouth, she wanted him too.

Long, sooty lashes swept her cheekbones and then lifted as her green eyes sparkled under the glittering bar-lights. The errant curl fell forward again, and this time restraint was beyond him. Reaching out, Jake caught the silky strands between his fingers and tucked them gently behind her ear. The slight contact sent lust roiling through his system as a shudder racked Cali's form. The muscles along her throat moved up and down, and her teeth set into her lush bottom lip, driving the breath out of his lungs. She didn't know what she was doing to him. Or maybe she did, and that was okay too.

Her gaze flitted back to his, uncertain and suddenly wary.

Hell. What was he doing? He had no business putting a move on a woman like her. She was sweet and sexy and a little bit shy. She wasn't the kind of woman you picked up for a night, or even a week's worth of nights, which was about the extent of what a guy like him had to offer.

"Jake," she half whispered, her voice barely audible above the sultry jazz pouring over them. "I'm not— When we started talking you were so funny and charming…I just figured a little flirting might be fun. I didn't mean for it to go anywhere. But you're so easy to talk to and I got carried away." Her gaze shifted off to the corner. "I'm sorry, I don't— I don't really…."

Cali turned aside, though he'd already seen the pretty blush that broke out across her cheekbones. Crooking a finger beneath her chin, he drew her gaze back to his.

"Hey, don't apologize. I know how to enjoy good conversation and a little flirting without it having to go back to a bedroom." Getting shut down really shouldn't have felt like a relief, but the way their small talk had wound its way into something deeper, more meaningful….

He liked her. And that was the problem. Jake didn't do meaningful.

She peered up at him through those dark lashes and his head began to spin. "It's just that maybe—"

A persistent vibration at his hip drew his attention from the woman in front of him to matters of life and death. "Hold that thought." With a reluctant shake of his head he pulled the phone from his pocket. "I'm sorry. This is the hospital. I've got to call in and check on a patient. Give me five minutes?"

She nodded. "Of course."

Cali watched as Jake made his way toward the back hall of the club, where a sign for the restrooms hung above the arched doorway. She needed to get out of there. Like, an hour ago. Her own stupidity was beyond belief. If Jake's phone hadn't interrupted— She didn't want to think about the words that had nearly sprinted off the tip of her tongue. The invitation—*agh*!

This man was beautiful in a cut-from-granite, his-maker-must-have-been-an-artist kind of way, and his physique alone was screwing with her head. What had begun as sporting flirtation had spiraled completely out of control into something more compelling than she was prepared to defend herself against.

It must be some kind of pheromone thing.

Definitely.

It was the clean, spicy scent of him drugging her senses that had her thinking in bad pick-up lines about a man she shouldn't have looked twice at. Let alone fallen into deep, lengthy, satisfying conversation with.

Cali sighed.

Just her bad luck he was interesting too. Intelligent and sharp, funny and thoughtful. Captivating in both mind and body. Far more dangerous than she'd realized.

She pushed her glass back on the bar and, clutching her purse, stood up. If she were smart, she'd haul it out of the club and straight into a cab before Jake got back. But that kind of insulting behavior wasn't in her. She'd run to the Ladies' Room and when she returned she'd thank him for a wonderful evening and leave. No exchange of phone numbers. No plans. A clear-cut goodbye.

Simple.

Only as she followed the series of switchbacks through the back hall of the club—past the Men's Room, then a door to the stage, and further on to the Ladies' Room—images of an easy smile and flashes of fathomless blue eyes began to chip at her resolve. At the end of the hall a sign glowed in neon blue for a phone, with an arrow pointing around the corner. Jake was probably down there and, for an instant, Cali considered following.

One night.

Really, what was the harm if she never saw him again? She'd been so very good, for so very long. Totally focused on work, completely dedicated….

Her gaze drifted down to the end of the hall, her body rebelling against her mind, until finally she pushed open the Ladies' Room door and stepped inside to splash some cold water on her face and some sense into her head.

CHAPTER TWO

IN THE relatively quiet back hall of the club, Jake ended the call about his bypass patient from that afternoon. Heading toward the main bar, he flipped the phone closed and glanced down as he pushed it into his pocket.

A slice of white light pierced the shadows just as Cali stepped out of the ladies' lounge and straight into his stride.

"Aack!" came her surprised yelp as their legs tangled together.

"Easy, I've got you," he assured her, catching her against him with one arm around her waist, the other braced at the wall.

Her palms covered his chest; her breasts and belly pressed against him so he could feel the rise and fall of her every tempting breath. One of them should have stepped away—put the distance back between them—but neither moved. Her gaze touched on his, hungry and aware, before drifting down to his mouth and holding as her lips parted on a trembling sigh. The air went thick with tension, and need surged to life, pumping hot through his veins, stifling reason.

The lounge door swung closed behind them, dropping the narrow hall into semi-darkness. It was intimate and secluded, and he wanted her. Every muscle tightened throughout his body, straining to take her. He wouldn't, but, watching the desperate flutter of her pulse at the hollow of her throat, he couldn't make himself step away either.

A tiny furrow etched between her brows as a single word pushed through her lips. "Don't."

Only Jake hadn't moved, hadn't given in. He was still holding himself in unrelenting check as he realized Cali hadn't been speaking to him, but to herself.

"Cali," he warned, something predatory responding to her weakening resolve. If she wanted to stop this, she'd have to tell *him* no. Only she didn't say anything. Didn't push him back. Instead her fingers curled into his sweater, her breath pulled ragged from her chest and the indecision faded from her eyes, taking his every good intention with it.

Cali's body shifted, soft and tempting against him in torturous slow motion, as she rose up on her toes and whispered, "Just one," before pressing her lips to his.

Sure, he thought, fighting a smile. No matter how good the intention, one would never be enough.

Slanting his mouth over hers in a smooth glide, deliberately light and teasing, he offered a kiss that hinted and lured, rather than taking outright.

Cali shuddered, her breath slipping over his lips with a soft moan that left every muscle in his body tensing, straining for more—but he could wait, because he knew it wouldn't be long. Splaying one hand against the base of her spine, he cupped her cheek with the other and pulled back to meet her gaze. "That good, huh?"

Her lips curved as she drank him in through half-lidded eyes. "I'd forgotten *just how good* that felt." The tip of her tongue darted out to moisten the sexy swell of her pink bottom lip. "It's been a really long time since I've been kissed."

Hell. He didn't want to think of her as vulnerable. Didn't want to like it. Not when that kind of knowledge, coupled with the husky quality her voice, was doing strange things to his ego, drawing out some inner need that damn near demanded he show her just what she'd been missing.

"Wasn't much of a kiss, if you ask me," he murmured. "I can do better."

Her eyes darkened like smoked sea glass and locked on his mouth, sending "go" signals toward his groin. Her breath hitched as, moving closer, he traced the smooth line of her delicate jaw with his thumb, sifted his fingers through the silky hair at the nape of her neck, and tilted her face to his.

"Maybe just one more," she whispered breathlessly, her lips an enticing invitation.

"One more," he agreed, intent on doling out a kiss with every skill and seductive nuance he'd honed since high school packed into it. And that kiss would become the prelude to a night in bed.

Jake's mouth descended on her yielding softness, sinking with a slow, steady build. A light back-and-forth rub. A gentle, parting pressure as his tongue sought the barest taste. She was warm and wet and teasing, fresh and inviting, and as her sultry sigh feathered against his mouth his smug satisfaction gave way to a rising need.

Her breathy gasps called like a plea for more and, angling his head to take control, he plunged his tongue between her lips. Lithe arms slipped around his neck and, delving into the warm depths of her mouth, he stroked in a wet velvet rub against her teeth, tongue and lips, thrusting and retreating in an erotic, suggestive rhythm.

Cali responded, clasping her arms tighter, molding her firm breasts and flat belly against his hips and chest.

Urgency ripped through him. His hand fisted in the fabric at the waist of her skirt and she moaned around his plundering tongue, a quiet, mewling sound that nearly had him yanking her skirt above her hips. Shocked by his own response, he tore away from the heated embrace. Stared down into Cali's flushed face.

He wanted her naked and beneath him the next time she made that sound.

Forcing the words out, he said, "Let's get out of here."

Breathless, she peered up at him, agony in her eyes. "I can't. I— Couldn't we—?" Her smoky gaze fixed on his mouth as the tightening in his gut became painful. "Just one minute more?"

The way her eyes went all warm and soft and needy—he'd have given her anything she asked for at that moment. He wanted to be inside her, but this gorgeous girl who hadn't been kissed for so long didn't want it to go that way. Hell, the strain of a few more minutes probably wouldn't kill him. And even if they did, it wouldn't be a bad way to go.

"Oh, yeah," he murmured, hauling her up against him so her feet lifted from the floor. He maneuvered them around the corner, to where the hinged door of the phone booth provided a modicum of privacy. Pulling her into the booth, barely large enough for them to stand side by side, he lowered his mouth to her ear. "Just one more minute."

Her fingers clutched at his shoulders as she pulled him back to her. "Thank God."

Cali was a woman possessed. It couldn't go further than this. She was treading on dangerous ground as it was, but, heaven help her, she couldn't give up the decadence of this stolen moment.

It might have been three years since she'd last been kissed, but she could say with all certainty she'd never in her life had a lip-lock like this one. A mind-numbing, moral-melting mainline into pleasure. His taste, touch and scent thrummed through her veins, so quickly and so thoroughly addictive the idea of breaking free was physically painful, mentally incomprehensible.

What harm could come from just a few more innocuous minutes of indulgence?

Strong hands ran in a crisscross down her back, until one wide palm pressed over her bottom, pulling her into closer contact with the hard contours of his body.

How could anything feel so right?

Grabbing her thighs, he hoisted her up. Her skirt bunched as her legs wrapped around his hips. Her shoulders braced against the wall as he rocked against that throbbing, long-neglected spot of need. Fingers of sensation stroked through her middle, tugging the strings of desire dangerously taut.

It was good. Too good to give up so fast. Just another minute like this and she'd stop. Leave. Run. But not yet.

"Oh, God!" she gasped when his hips ground forward again, rasping rough denim and damp lace against her achy sex.

Some distant part of her mind screamed a frantic warning.

She had rules about this sort of thing.

But their position was too perfect, the contact just right, and she was halfway to satisfaction already.

Jake's mouth tore free from her lips, his blue flame gaze searing over her as his breath punched free in ragged bursts. "Tell me to stop," he gritted out, his hips moving in a steady rhythm so good she couldn't have told him to stop if her life had depended on it.

On some level she knew he was right. One of them was going to have to come to their senses, and instinctively she understood the burden fell on her shoulders. But why the hell did it always have to be the girl?

As exciting and amazing as it was, they were in a bar.

In a phone booth.

Her eyes blinked open, her gaze flitting over the small confines of their space.

A phone booth with a wooden shuttered and hinged door that ran almost floor to ceiling.

A phone booth at the farthest end of a scarcely traveled, dimly lit switchback hallway. With Jake's broad, powerful back a further shield against any prying eyes should someone actually venture this far.

She'd never see this man again. No one would ever know.

Jake's lean male hips ground forward again, his head bowed and his lips pulled at the vulnerable skin beneath her ear, shredding her resolve.

And then all she could think was that they were alone. With the female singer's smooth molasses voice pouring over them from the speakers above, and the space around them fading into nothing more than a hazy backdrop for this single stolen moment. His teeth grazed the column of her neck, and one hand caught her wrist to pin it at the wall beside her head. Her body seized; her mind blanked of anything beyond giving in.

She clutched at him with her knees. Rocked her hips to meet his and desperately sought his mouth with her own. Lips fused together, their tongues tangled, mated, and merged. Their mouths were completing the act clothing barely re-stricted lower on their bodies. So intimate. She could taste him. Feel him thrusting and licking inside her.

She could wrap herself in his strength. Lose herself in his control.

And then he stopped, held her still as she teetered at the brink of a precipice she couldn't believe she'd been brought to. Her breath fired in moist bursts between them as tension gripped her with stunning intensity, leaving her helpless, des-perate, shaking with need.

"Jake." The plea in that single husky word was unmistak-able, and she felt his answering smile curl against her ravaged mouth. Oh, yes.

"Come for me." His low growl stroked like a vibration deep through her body and soul, curling around the tender spot between her legs just as he rocked again, letting her ride the steely length of him in one long, brutal caress that unlocked her every inhibition.

Spasms of hot pleasure lanced her core, relentless and intense. Stealing her breath through each ratcheting increment until at last it burst free with her shuddering release. Jake caught her fleeting cries with his kiss, held her steady in his arms as her body melted against him. Seconds ticked by as she floated in blissful oblivion. Then slowly her mind cleared and reality descended with the resounding thud of Jake's back hitting the phone behind him.

Cali's eyes blinked open.

A bar.

A phone booth, for heaven's sake!

A stranger.

No. Of all the wrongs piled into one grotesquely cheap heap in Cali's mind, Jake Tyler wasn't one of them. She might have met him only hours ago, but something about the man spoke to her on a level she couldn't deny. He was the kind of guy she could fall for—if she were in the market for falling. Which she wasn't.

Jake's brow, damp from restraint or exertion, or possibly a combination of the two, pressed against hers as he stood, eyes closed, shaking his head. "I feel like a teenager." He didn't sound upset so much as stunned.

She smiled her understanding—not that she'd actually ever done anything even remotely like this when she was in high school, but she would have liked to. "I think you had more fun as a teen than I did."

Jake chuckled, that low and sexy sound that made her wonder if maybe—

No. Tonight was an exception.

A brief foray into fantasy. A depraved one-night indulgence she was certain she *should* already want to forget. Only it had been too good to forget. And, with her work cut out for her with MetroTrek, the memory of this night would probably have to keep her warm for the next few years at least.

Seeing how completely Jake affected her was reason enough to keep her libido in check and an incentive to make a hasty exit. Though not too hasty, because she didn't want to seem ungrateful.

She was grateful, all right. Was she ever!

But Jake— Well, neither exchanging numbers nor getting busted for lewd behavior in the back of a bar held much allure for her. It was extraction time from this sticky situation. The man who had so generously withheld his own release, and now ran his big sexy hands over her hips to smooth the wrinkles from her skirt, needed to become a fond memory she'd never have to see again.

She didn't know what to say, how to get out of the phone booth and back to her life. "Um, thank you. That was—"

"A better kiss?" he asked, flashing the easy smile that had gotten her into this situation in the first place.

"You're a charmer."

He brushed his thumb over her cheek. "Yeah, and you're standing on my foot."

Cali jerked back, coming up short against the booth wall, before righting herself with the help of Jake's hand at her waist. "Sorry."

"Not a problem, but we should probably get out of this booth before some schmuck's phone battery dies and our luck runs out."

She glanced up at the ceiling, feeling the flush of embarrassment heating her cheeks. "Flee the scene of the crime and all?"

Jake caught her chin with a crook of his finger and tilted her face to look at him. "I'll take you home so we can do this right." His gaze held steady, intense and hungry.

Her breath hitched at the thought of what he could do on a bed, if given the chance.

"Jake, I can't have a relationship."

He shook his head, letting out an ironic laugh. "And, trust me, I can't give you one. But tonight…I could give you tonight."

Just one night?

A quiet ping sounded from the floor, piercing the lust-induced fog of her brain. Oh, no, it was a message alert from her phone. The phone so carelessly dumped with her clutch on the floor when her hormones had skidded out of control on a collision course with Jake.

Her link to Amanda, to her job, to her future, was a hair's breadth from being trampled! A few hours with this man and her focus was shot. What if she gave him a full night? She already knew the answer to that. It wouldn't be enough. With a man like Jake she would want more.

She kicked the small bag out of the booth toward the safety of the abandoned hall, and then, forcing the air from her lungs, pulled free of his gentle hold and voiced the words that would hurt to say. "I can't. I'm sorry."

Jake's brows drew down, his features hardening as he inched back to let her pass. "Cali, wait—hold on."

She shook her head, scooping up the bag with her phone and holding them close to her chest. "I wish—" But that wouldn't do any good. Pinching her lips between her teeth, still tasting him on her tongue, she shook her head and ran from the club as if temptation itself was on her heels.

CHAPTER THREE

AWARENESS crept in, staking daylight's claim over her consciousness, shooing away the hazy bliss of midnight's oblivion. Within her hotel room, Cali fixed her gaze on the ceiling above her.

She'd done it in a phone booth. Almost.

In the deserted back hall of a jazz club.

With a man she'd just met.

It was *totally* a one-night stand.

Okay, so she hadn't had *actual* sex. A technicality. They'd been standing. And it had been one night. One incredible night, topped off with an incredible kiss that flamed so far out of control it had passed X-rated—and by the time it finished, so had she.

Wow. It definitely counted.

A one-night stand. Something "good girls" were supposed to regret. Not wake the next day feeling refreshed, rejuvenated, and all around delighted to have cast their morals aside.

The "morning after" was supposed to be a miserable, hollow, shame-ridden experience. She'd heard it from a variety of reliable sources. But by the time she'd found her shoulders braced against the wall of the tiny phone booth, with Jake's kiss coursing through her veins, she'd been more than willing to accept the consequences.

Only now, snuggled into her so recently sated skin, Cali couldn't seem to muster even a smidgeon of remorse. Maybe she'd get there someday, but as of this glorious morning Jake Tyler had been the best exception to a rule she'd ever made.

After a three-year self-imposed dry spell, he'd been just the kind of no promises, no risks, no regrets tall-glass-of-water Cali hadn't even realized she'd been thirsting for. And now, quenched as she was, she could take on the Chicago assignment and knock the ball right out of Wrigley Field.

Finding a spot of too-cool sheets, she curled into herself, pulling the heavenly comforter tight and letting her mind slip back to the night before. To the deep blue-eyed gaze that had kept her pinned to her seat for hours longer than she'd planned to stay out. The warm, easy laugh that had slipped past her defenses and sent unexpected heat swirling low in her belly.

That rapturous kiss.

God, his mouth was phenomenal.

And the rest. Yum.

Still staring at the ceiling, Cali let out a wistful sigh.

No-harm recreation at its best. The one-night distraction by tall, dark and devastating had been sensational.

She should be ashamed, but couldn't quite summon the energy for it. She'd never see him again. There was zero chance of *this man* ruining her career. It was bittersweet perfection.

At least it would be if she could forget the look on his face when she'd run like a fool from the club.

Flopping the comforter back with a groan, she emerged from her warm cocoon.

Shake it off.

A quick glance at the clock told her Amanda's beloved

brother-in-law was due within the hour, to take her over to her new place.

Her teeth set as she blew out a steady breath. Time to shift gears and get moving.

Stepping into the shower, she hoped the hot spray and lemon-sage lather of shampoo would wash her mind clean of all things Jake—there wasn't time to get caught up in a crush, no matter how gorgeous or funny or intelligent— No! The man's pure perfection stemmed from the fact that he'd been little more than a ship passing in the night.

Wait, not a ship. A sleek, sexy speed boat, whose wake had rocked her world.

Sure. Just one kiss. What was the harm in one tiny kiss after three years of going without?

Ha. Well, now she knew.

There would be no forgetting him.

She toweled off, with images of glinting eyes and a hard-planed chest pressed against her teasing her resolve. Ponderings of how different her life might have been if she'd been with a man like Jake three years ago in Boston instead of with Erik.

That was nonsense. When Jake had asked to take her home, she'd fled from the man. Imagining him in her life in any capacity other than as the exciting one-night spectacular exception he'd been was crazy. She wouldn't. Definitely not. No matter how much he'd made her laugh. Want.

Agitated, she jammed her legs into a pair of jeans, then pulled a periwinkle and white halter over her head. As if in accordance with her mood, her curls had gone particularly wild that morning, requiring that she gather them at the nape of her neck with a leather tie. A dab of lipgloss and done. Satisfied with her look, she was just tossing back a glass of water when three hard knocks sounded at the hotel door.

A smile broke out across her face as excitement welled within her. Forget about blue-eyed bar heroes. On the other side of that door was Amanda's brother-in-law, Jackson, here to deliver her to the rest of her life—or at least to the sublet where she'd live while she worked her butt off nailing this job for Amanda. It was go-time.

Barefoot, glass in hand, she darted over to the door and pulled it open wide. "Hey, give me one minute…."

The rest of her words died on her tongue as she gasped at the sight of Jake Tyler, casual in worn denim and a cuffed button-down, leaning with one arm braced against the frame of her door.

His brow drew down as his darkening eyes took her in. "You?"

Cali stood immobile, dread hollowing the pit of her stomach. It was a mistake. It couldn't be what it looked like— Jake wasn't *Jackson.*

Oh, God. Her boss's little sister's husband. Lying about his name while he scored in a bar!

No!

Breath ratcheting, she staggered back.

She could *not* have screwed up again. Not this quickly; not this royally! Maybe she was wrong and this was some kind of happy misunderstanding. Maybe Jake was just some sick stalker, bent on creeping her out with his ability to track her. Maybe he wasn't her boss's brother-in-law after all.

Let it be true, she prayed, willing to offer him a pair of her panties, or whatever insane keepsake he wanted, so long as he didn't confirm that she'd been swapping spit with the married man her boss secretly coveted.

"Jackson?" she whispered, clinging to the hope that he'd shake his head and deny it, come after her with a knife instead.

The corner of a mouth she'd had her lips all over turned

up the slightest degree. "*No one* calls me Jackson but Amanda and my mother."

No apologies, no denials, no miraculous explanation proving she hadn't blown everything before she'd even gotten through the gate. Just that calmly assessing gaze, smug and secure. Amused, even. What could he possibly find amusing about this situation?

The backs of her knees collided with the low coffee table behind her before she realized she was still retreating—and momentum kept her going.

"Aiyee!" Her arms flailed, then she shot one out to catch herself. Instead, the glass in her hand broke the fall, crushed in her palm as her rear-end smacked down.

Glass shards glittered pink as they drowned in the rising wash of blood at her wrist. "Ungg…." she moaned. "Cut myself…." Jake's guttural curse registered vaguely as he appeared, crouching at her side. The room dimmed, tilting, and distorted images began playing before her eyes.

Of course it wasn't her life flashing there—she wasn't dying. Merely fainting from the sight of her own blood. No, the images she saw were a series of memories, bar-side snapshots, leading to her latest life-shattering, career-flushing mistake.

"Ah, hell." Jake muttered, quickly assessing the injury. "Not too bad, but we need to get the glass out."

Cali let out a sick moan. As his focus shot to her paling face, and her eyes fixed on the blood oozing down her arm, he knew without question what was next. "No. Don't look at it, sweetheart…. No—no, don't—" Too late. Her eyes rolled back, her face went slack, and her body crumpled against him. *Great.*

This just got better and better.

The last thing he'd expected as he knocked on the hotel room door was for the incredible woman who'd run out on him the night before to open it. But once it had happened, and he'd seen who she was—connecting Cali to Calista—he'd indulged in a momentary fantasy about picking things up where they'd left off.

Obviously he was going to have to forget about that ego-driven idiocy, because Cali clearly hadn't been thinking the same thing. In those first seconds she'd looked more like she wanted to skin him than screw him, so it was safe to assume she was annoyed to discover he wasn't just some stranger who'd gotten her off and then conveniently faded into the mist. And that didn't jibe with the image he'd constructed from the night before. Which was just irritating. She'd been soft. Funny. Sweet. And a little bit shy, blushing at her own interest.

He'd spent hours lost in her laughter.

He was an idiot.

He did *not* want a relationship. And he did *not* date—even in his *über*-casual capacity—women connected to his family. Ever. They came with too many strings that were too hard to sever, and he wasn't interested in the complications. So why should it matter if Cali wasn't exactly who he'd thought the night before? If what had happened wasn't quite as special as he'd thought?

It shouldn't—didn't.

And *special*? What was he? Twelve? They'd been in a phone booth, for God's sake.

But she *was* now crumpled in his arms, and he *did* care about getting her cleaned up and back on her feet. Pulling her into his chest, he banded one arm behind her back and the other beneath her knees, then swept her up.

"Cali? Calista, sweetheart?"

Dodging the low-profile furniture in the suite, he crossed to the bathroom and sat with her tucked into his lap, her arm elevated, head lolling against his chest as she struggled to come around.

"Hey," he whispered into the top of her hair. "Don't

watch—just look up at me or keep your eyes closed while I wash this out."

But in the mirror's reflection he saw her eyes on the sink, where the water was tinged with red as he ran the tap over her arm…and she was out again. The cuts were shallow and didn't require stitches, so he finished up, then carried her to the bed. He laid Cali back, using a towel to protect the rumpled spread.

Blood rose slowly on her cuts—but it was nothing a few Band-Aids wouldn't take care of. At the very least they'd cover enough to keep Cali conscious. He returned to the bathroom and, with only mild guilt, began riffling through her bags. In his experience women traveled with enough toiletries to perform a double bypass, so Band-Aids were a sure bet.

In addition to a selection of cosmetics, brushes, sprays, gels and creams, he noted the slim case of her birth control pills, a pack of breath mints, mouthwash, floss and, in one stiff zippered plastic compartment, a single condom with a label he hadn't seen since med school. The expiration date had passed the year before.

Somehow the idea of Cali packing her little wash bag with the accoutrements of a sexually responsible woman—even though it appeared she'd had limited or lack-luster experience if that one single condom had suffered such a bleak and joyless existence in her bag—made him think again of the way she'd looked at him the night before as she confessed that she hadn't been kissed in such a very long time.

He shouldn't be thinking about it. The way she'd melted against him, the taste of her sigh in his mouth, the heat of her—

This was Amanda's new shooting star. He didn't want the strings. But still he made a mental note that if Cali ever looked at him as she had last night—if his resolve ever weakened—to bring his own protection. A whole box, not a single rubber.

Behind the decrepit prophylactic he hit the jackpot, with a small stash of equally ancient bandages. Returning to Cali's side, he peeled the adhesive backs free then carefully applied them to cover her cuts.

"Pretty big faint for not a lot of wound, there, Cali." He pushed a lock of hair from her eyes, tracing down the line of her jaw and under it to the soft, warm skin of her neck, where he found her carotid artery. Her pulse beat against the gentle pressure of his fingers, healthy and strong.

As he stared down at her face he saw she was beginning to stir. Her long-lashed lids fluttered like butterfly wings and then slowly lifted, revealing eyes like emeralds. Her lips parted, and he had the insane urge to sink into them with a kiss—

"Get your filthy hands off me."

Jake arched a brow, not bothering to fight the smile that rose in response to her throaty grunt. "My hands are clean, sweetheart. Habit of the trade. Aren't you a nasty little ogre in the morning?"

Cali began pushing up on her good arm, her sharp-edged stare slashing at him, but Jake stopped her with a firm hand against her shoulder and pushed her back into the mattress. "Not yet. Let's give it a minute more before you hop out of bed. Do you always faint at the sight of blood?"

Her jaw flexed, and a sound that was almost a growl emanated from low in her throat. "Only when it's mine. Your blood wouldn't bother me a bit."

For someone on the edge of consciousness, her temper seemed in good working order. Jake leaned back, amused. "Really? Interesting."

"Not interesting. Not interested. I'm furious, so thanks for catching me, but back off."

Wow. "Take it easy. My presence on your bed is purely professional. Doctor? Remember?"

Cali's delicate jaw clenched as she blew out an angry breath and refused to meet his eyes.

"Someone must have gotten under your skin good. Look, I didn't know you worked for Amanda, but, honestly, does it really matter now?" From the look of her scowl, Jake gathered it did.

"Are you kidding?" Cali gritted out, flashing him a murderous glare.

"This is because of last night?" he asked, confused by the overt hostility. "Or did I miss something else?"

Maybe she was as worried about Amanda as he was. But her lashing out at him didn't make a world of sense. It was an accident. One of fate's little mess-ups you lived with and got past.

If she was *miffed* he could understand it. Sulking or in a bit of a pout, sure. Women got that way. But Cali wasn't any of those. She looked as though she wanted to flay him alive. Considering he'd just carried her, princess-style, across her suite while she dripped blood down his sleeve, and then spent the next five minutes cleaning her minor but messy wounds, a smidgeon of gratitude seemed in order. But, no, she was in a snit.

Emotional *and* unreasonable, he thought with an inward shiver. Yeah, definitely no more kissing. Right about now he was wishing last night hadn't taken place either. Being tied, however loosely, to a woman with an irrational temper wasn't high on his list. Add in the complication of Amanda having a vested interest in this woman's happiness and productivity, and things could get awkward.

It wouldn't be fair to any of them. Time to neutralize the situation. Bring in some reason. "Look, I know you're angry," he began in an appeasing tone, reminded again of why superficial non-relationships so suited him. "This is an uncomfortable situation for both of us. Last night we had a moment together, and today, all things considered, it's clearly a *good thing* that it didn't go any further than it did. Really, what happened is no big deal."

A fair acknowledgment on his part.

"No big deal?" Her lip curled in distaste.

"Okay, maybe that was rude," he muttered, the dread he associated with unreasonable women setting in. What was he supposed to say?

CHAPTER FOUR

CALI felt her stomach congeal. "Talk about an understatement."

"Yeah, well…." Jake's jaw shifted, his mouth pulling to the side as he watched her for a second and then shrugged. "It is what it is."

Excuse me? She pushed up to her elbows to glare at him. What the hell did *that* mean? The man had just been caught cheating. How dared he be so blasé? This was bad for her— of that there was no doubt. But for Jake? Didn't he *care* that his marriage was at stake?

"Anyway, do you need some help with your bags?" he asked, obviously wanting to wrap up the encounter as quickly as possible.

Please. "Oh, I think you've done enough already," she bit out, her panic and temper on the rise. It took everything she had not to kick his two-timing shin.

To think she'd been fantasizing about this guy, aching for more of him…and he was *married*! He'd made *her* the *other woman*. Her instincts stank. She flopped back on the bed, and to her horror tears began to well at the corners of her eyes.

"Cali," he said from the door. His voice low, oozing under-standing. *Manipulator.* "I can see you're—"

With a tight shake of her head, she threw up a hand to cut him off. "No. Not a word."

She felt weak, as though the disappointment was physically weighing her down. And it wasn't just over him. Sure, Jake was gorgeous—even being a disgusting pig of a cheater couldn't take that away. But it was his personality as much as his incredible eye-candy appeal she'd found so attractive.

It hurt to be so wrong about him. But, more than being disappointed in who he was, she was disappointed in herself. Three years of keeping her nose clean. Of focusing on work to the exclusion of all else. Of not even giving a man the time of day. And the very first one she decided to give a little flirt to was married.

Her stomach dropped.

To her boss's sister.

So much for a harmless tryst. She couldn't think of a single person who wouldn't be hurt here.

Okay, damage control time. She hadn't known Jake was Jackson or she would have run for her life. But, even so, she didn't see Amanda being all that understanding. Obviously it would be in Jake's best interests to keep the sordid details on the down-low. But what about her? Could she live with herself if she didn't confess what had happened—if she knowingly participated in the deception of another woman? Sure, they might not have had actual intercourse, but it wasn't because Jake had thrown up a hand and said no way. He'd been ready to go. He'd wanted to take her home—back to her place, of course.

Oh, he was scum.

No, she definitely could not live with that kind of secret. Even if it meant she'd be sacrificing London—her career. And there was every chance that was exactly what this tawdry little rendezvous had cost her. Because Amanda wasn't a machine. She was a flesh-and-blood human being, with emotions, who might not be able to put *reason* ahead of *hurt*.

Why hadn't she just walked out of the bar last night? With her track record, why had she pushed her luck and let a man get that close at all? Hadn't she learned how easily men came between her and her future?

This one was trouble, Jake thought, meeting the flash of Cali's cold stare. She shifted and her bound curls caught the light streaming through the window, making the soft mass gleam like gilded silk. And for a moment he could see it wound around his fist, thick between his fingers as he pulled her head back.

That was the wrong line of thinking, considering he'd decided she was off-limits. And she'd decided he was an ass.

But, even with a disdainful sneer marring her lips, she made a pretty picture. Faded jeans hugged the sexy lines of her trim hips. A sleeveless shirt was tied behind her neck and ruffled out, accentuating her lean, athletic build, as well as the natural curves he'd had pressed against him all too briefly the night before. Her body was fit, with an arsenal of feminine dips, hollows and swells—enough to make any man's mouth water.

She was a siren, all right. And at that moment a particularly hateful looking one. Of course the outrage might have something to do with the blatant full-body assessment he'd just concluded.

"Nice," she hissed.

He *was* an ass. "Sorry," he acknowledged, with an unrepentant smile.

Cali's eyes rolled. "Right. Whatever." Scrunching up her face like a raisin, she fisted her hands against her eyes, muttering, "Stupid, stupid…. One night—*sure*, no problem… stupid. *Stupid*!"

Jake raised his brows at her self-directed tirade, concerned by the intensity of her dismay. That was until she spun on him.

"And you—you're the epitome of every bar-side scavenger I've ever heard about. You revolt me!"

Jake stiffened, his concern rapidly evaporating under the

scalding lash of her tongue. "What?" *Scavenger*? Man, that got under his skin. And he *revolted* her? This from the woman who had begged him for just one more kiss? "Were you even *there* last night?" No wonder she hadn't gotten much lip action lately—she was insane.

Glaring daggers, she snapped, "To my eternal regret."

Where in the hell was her outrage coming from? This couldn't be the same woman who'd tied him up in knots and nearly brought him to his knees. He didn't understand—and he *hated* that.

He waited for enlightenment to smack his forehead.

It didn't.

There had to be an answer. "Are you on drugs?"

"Get lost, *Jackson*."

And now with the *Jackson* business? Nice. *Yeah, you first.* "Seriously, Cali, what's your problem?"

Her head snapped around. "Are you kidding?"

He rolled his shoulders, then cocked his head, waiting her out. She issued a disgusted grunt and blew a renegade tendril of hair from her eyes with an exasperated breath. "I work for your sister-in-law. And, as I'm sure you're aware, a position within her corporation is highly coveted."

Jake watched her march around the hotel room, gathering her things. "Yeah. I'm aware."

As a rule he considered himself a gentleman, but he'd be damned if he'd help—especially since her arm didn't seem to be bothering her too much and the dressing was holding. Instead he propped a shoulder against the wall, crossing his arms and legs, and forced a careless smile while refusing to give in to the urge to grab that bag out of her hands and load it himself.

Cali wrenched a zipper closed, huffing. "So you see what's at stake?"

Not really. Aside from the fact that what had happened last

night had nothing to do with Cali's job, Jake was a big boy, and not prone to crowing about his phone booth conquests to just anyone who would listen. If *she* wasn't planning to spill to Amanda, Jake was more than happy to save himself a whole lot of hassle and keep his mouth shut too.

Only Cali was back in his face, panic and fury blazing in her cheeks. "I see that smug look," she accused, like the crazy person he suspected her to be. "Don't think for one second that you have me bent over a barrel because of last night."

Bent over a barrel?

Right now she deserved to be bent over his knee. His jaw clenched as he struggled for patience. What did it matter what she thought? Jake wasn't a man concerned with others' perceptions, so why should he feel himself rising to the bait of this woman he had nothing, *nothing*, invested in?

She glared up at him in silent accusation, and suddenly concepts like self-control and maturity lost their allure. "Relax, sweetheart, if I'd really wanted you in bed, or bent over anything, I would have had you there last night. All I had to do was stop one second earlier and you would have been begging me. Strike that. You *did* beg."

Cali's chin pulled back with her gasp. Patches of red splashed up her neck and face. "You jackass!"

Ha! That felt better. Rising above was overrated. "Really? Me?"

"I never—"

"Please, don't even try to deny that you weren't desperate for what I gave you."

Cali's fists landed on her hips as she leaned forward. "Desperate's a pretty big word when satisfaction comes as easy as a pack of D-cell batteries, buddy," she answered with an icy laugh.

He knew what she was implying, and he didn't want to

think about it—not now. Not with her waving her ticket to Crazyville in his face.

They'd gotten off track, anyway. Closing his eyes, he gritted his teeth for a moment's control. They needed to take this down a notch.

"Look, trust me, I'm not about to go talking to Amanda about this."

"Oh, *that* I never doubted," she huffed. "Men like you make me want to…to…."

She'd stopped in her tracks, and, standing there red-faced, arms cocked at her sides, fists balled, she looked as if she wanted to stomp her foot.

She was a hassle.

Irrational.

Probably bipolar, considering the swing from last night's engaging sweetheart to this morning's unreasonable aggressor. His focus narrowed on the rise and fall of her chest, the pull and give of blue and white fabric across her breasts, the flush of red that darkened the hollow between them.

Sexy.

Jake didn't do "crazy". The passionate drama that drew some men was, to him, like a neon sign flashing in screaming orange: *Run!*

Only this time it wasn't.

This time all that irrational heat and intensity was wrapped in a package he'd had his hands on once and was finding it harder and harder to ignore.

"Men like me make you want to what?" he asked, taking a step toward her, dropping his tone to a bedroom lure. "I know what I made you want last night."

"Low-life bastard." Her breath came faster, and the flutter of her pulse beneath the delicate skin of her neck became frantic. When she stepped back he closed in, propelled by some kind of contagious mental illness driving his predatory urge.

"Tell me, Cali. What's so different about this morning?" he taunted.

Her eyes darkened, the long muscles of her throat moving up and down as she backed herself into the wall, crossing her arms over her chest—but not fast enough to hide the evidence of her hardened nipples straining through the taut fabric of her shirt. Lies and denial would only take her so far.

"Are you deranged?" she whispered, in a husky voice that betrayed her emotions as much as the rest of her body had.

Definitely. He had to be. Because something inside him had snapped and all he could think about was getting Cali into that big bed behind her. "You respond to me physically. I can see it."

"Because you're man-candy. But I still wouldn't touch you with a ten-foot pole."

"Man-candy?" He nearly laughed, loving the sound of it. "Really?"

"It's an insult!" she hissed, shaking her head in disbelief. "I'm dehumanizing you. Feel cheap and dirty, but for God's sake don't revel in it!"

There wasn't much he could do but shrug. "Man-candy" was the best insult he'd heard this decade. But Cali wasn't done with him.

"Is this some kind of sexual addiction condition with you? Do you need a support group? Can I call your sponsor?"

Jake just stared steadily at her, knowing the bravado was about to break. And then it did—only not in the breathless, tossing-herself-into-his-arms way he'd expected.

Suddenly Cali looked weary and defeated as she peered up at him. "Don't vows mean anything to you?"

That stopped him dead. *Vows?*

Pieces of the puzzle began to fall into place, revealing a picture—

Not possible. She couldn't think….

But then it all made sense. The way she'd referred to Amanda. Her shock at seeing him, her hostility, her disgust, her resistance to the obvious chemistry between them.

She thought he was married. And she was utterly undone over it—out of her mind upset, offended, and enraged.

The corner of his mouth pulled into a grin he couldn't fight. His sexy Cali, who hadn't been kissed in so very long and who sparked his blood to fire, was a principled little thing.

"Stop leering at me like that!" she snapped.

"So this—this animosity is about the vows?" he asked, suddenly curious about the strength of her convictions.

She blinked twice, and then met his stare with her own. "Don't mock me. Of course it's about the vows. And my job. Amanda's my boss. It's despicable that you don't have enough respect for your poor wife to keep your tongue to yourself."

"Hey, as I remember it, you seemed rather eager for my tongue last night." And she'd tasted good, too.

"But to drag me into your—your debauchery is unconscionable—"

Debauchery? Come on, that was cute.

"Of course if you don't care about your marriage, why would I think you'd care about jeopardizing my career?"

Now, that wasn't something she should have to worry about. This had gone far enough.

"Just settle down. You've got me all wrong—" he began, feeling better than he had since the moment she tore out of the bar.

"Save it. I haven't *got* you at all." With a cock of her head and a patronizing smile, she added, "Nor do I have any desire to get you."

"No, Cali, really, you—"

"Please! I'm not interested. If you'll give me the key and the address, we can say goodbye now and get on with the fallout from this freaking disaster." Her fury seemed to burn away as he watched. She slumped against the wall, her face slackened and her lids closed. "Please."

Jake caught her chin between his finger and thumb and forced her to look at him. "Let me finish."

Sure he had her attention, he softened his voice and lowered his face an inch closer to hers. "I didn't realize Amanda still referred to me as her brother-in-law, because, lawfully speaking, I'm not. The 'poor wife' you're referring to remarried four years ago, and has been living quite happily with Paulo ever since."

Her mouth dropped open, making Jake's curve.

"I. Am. Not. Married."

CHAPTER FIVE

MOUTH dry, head swimming, Cali stared dumbly. "You're divorced?"

"I prefer single," he offered, with an all too amused wink. "It has a more pristine ring to it."

She'd just verbally assaulted the starring member in the hottest memory of her life, humiliated herself with gross misunderstanding, and there Jake stood, as stylish and smooth as the sleek hotel room itself, arms crossed, staring at her expectantly. Waiting for an apology, she supposed. Deserving one, possibly. Probably.

Finally, she let out a huff and reluctantly met his eyes. "This is awkward."

"Isn't it, though?" Again with that smirk.

So he wasn't married. That was good. But somehow the knowledge did little to alleviate her tension as his gaze slipped down to her mouth and then back up to her eyes.

That was bad.

She might not have earned the unsavory title of Other Woman, but she wasn't out of the woods. "Amanda still thinks of you as her sister's husband." Or possibly she'd earmarked him as intended for her own use. Either way, mouth-staring was a serious breach of etiquette.

"I assure you, she does not." He sounded confident, but men could be obtuse when it came to seeing, or not seeing, what was right in front of their faces. Like a sister-in-law's crush.

Cali needed to look away, because the arrogant curve of those lips she'd test driven the night before was doing things to body parts that wanted in on the action.

No!

Regardless of Jake's proven ability to deliver on the promises he was making without words, she shouldn't be eyeing him as anything more than a ride to her new place. He was off-limits.

"Settle down, Cali. We didn't actually sleep together, so you can stop hyperventilating and turning beet-red every minute and a half."

"I am not—" Clearing her throat, she glanced down at the carpet, across to the low-profile coffee table and couch, then up to the recessed lighting. Anywhere but into his eyes. Suddenly that shame she hadn't been able to muster a mere hour ago was on hand and in abundance. She'd *begged* Amanda's brother-in-law for kisses. Revealed her desperation by admitting to how long she'd been without. And then used him until she—oh, the humiliation.

"How's that feeling?"

Her head snapped up to see Jake jut his chin toward her injured arm.

Cali glanced down, almost surprised by the patchwork of Band-Aids. "It's fine, thanks." Honestly, it barely registered. "I suppose I owe you an apology."

His thumbs hooked into the pockets of his jeans. "We both jumped to conclusions. Let's just forget about it."

That seemed fair, but with his body so close to hers she wasn't exactly thinking straight. Which had her temper kicking back into gear. "Why didn't you just tell me?" she demanded.

"That I was divorced?" He chuckled, shaking his head. "It

didn't come up last night and I didn't realize you thought I was married this morning. Why didn't *you* just ask?"

"Amanda calls you her brother-in-law. She raves about you—and I've never even heard of this Paulo before."

"Well, Amanda and I have been friends since we were kids. More like family, really, even back then. And she doesn't particularly care for Paulo, though as far as I know he's a decent guy."

The whole situation was absurd, and yet Jake was staring down at her, his Prince-Charming-gone-bad smile spreading by the minute. Irritating her. She was writhing with discomfort and he looked immensely entertained. The nerve! "Are you having fun?"

Something in his expression turned serious. His endlessly blue gaze washed over her, drawing her in deeper as his fingers moved to the side of her face, brushing lightly over her cheekbones. His chest rose on a long, slow inhalation before he answered. "Not nearly as much as I'd like to."

The air was charged. Suddenly the comfortable suite Cali had spent the night in felt claustrophobic and confining. Her breath sucked in as Jake closed the distance between them. She should stop him, say something, only her mind had disconnected from the body that leaned forward, aching to touch. A million things ran through her mind. Laughter and need. Frustration and desire. Tastes and textures from the night before that made her mouth water and her pulse jump.

His lips stopped a scant breath from hers. Their eyes locked, held.

"Just one." It was neither question nor command. Just the deep rasp of Jake's warning an instant before his mouth closed over hers.

She should have been able to resist. Pull away. Turn her head. At the very least ride it out with stoic indifference and a stiff lip. Anything! Except the familiar blade of his tongue teasing the seam of her lips—the coaxing pressure of a kiss barely begun—had her opening to him, trembling. Lost. Instantly desperate for his taste. Her body heated, tightened and went lax all at once as he slipped between her teeth. Stroked slow and deep, and dragged a helpless moan from the depths of her desire.

Jake angled his head, and she melted against the hard planes of his body, let him fill her with his claim. Gave in to the heady rush of energy that surged like molten desire through her veins. It burned and branded, scorched with an irresistible heat that made her want to scream. *More.*

His hands moved over her, hot and demanding, pushing over the swell of her breast, teasing the beaded tip of her nipple with his palm, grasping the base of her bottom to pull her closer to the hardening contours of his body. Hungry lips pulled at the tender skin beneath her jaw, found her earlobe and sucked. "What is it about you?" he growled into her curls.

Her breath coming in ragged bursts, Cali's eyes opened as his gruff demand penetrated her psyche. What was it about *him*? Last night had been an honest mistake, but today there was no excuse. She knew who he was. Knew he was Amanda's… Amanda's… Well, whatever he was, he was Amanda's. Or at least that was how her boss saw it, which was all that should matter to Cali.

She pushed at Jake's shoulders. Tried not to think about replacing her hands with her mouth to nip at the solid muscle beneath. "Jake. This is a mistake."

His gaze bored into her. If he'd sunk back into the kiss she would have been lost. Utterly. But instead he searched her face, her eyes. Holding her rapt until the smoky hunger dissipated and once again the clear blue sky stared down at her. "You're probably right about that."

Cali nodded, still unable to look away, still held in arms so strong and secure she'd nearly melted in them.

His lips brushed against her temple and then he pulled back, his face composed, pleasant. Unreadable. "Let's get you over to your new place."

Top down, radio off, Jake rolled to a stop beneath the hotel's awning. He'd gone for the car while Cali organized the last of her files and folders and checked out, allowing him a moment to get a grip on the uncharacteristic impulses laying siege to his brain and various organs to the south.

Neither of them needed the complications jumping into bed would raise. Rationally, he knew that. Only it seemed his response to Cali wasn't entirely rational.

Gripping the black leather-encased wheel, he shut his eyes and tried to ground himself. Women didn't go to his head like this. Ever. Sure, he was susceptible to their allure in a general, appreciative kind of way, but he was a pragmatic guy. He didn't do the stupid thing. Didn't throw caution aside for a good time—not anymore. Life had consequences. It was a lesson he'd learned the hard way a long time ago, and one he didn't forget. So why was he even thinking about a woman who A: kept turning him away, and B: came with strings?

Well, the answer to A didn't take a rocket scientist to figure out. Her reluctance to get involved made her safe. She wasn't interested in a relationship—she'd said it flat out at the bar—and yet she couldn't quite resist him. So he wouldn't have to worry about her planning their wedding the first time he got her into a bed. Which made her ideally suited for a fling. Throw in the fact that she was leaving within a few months' time and it *almost* negated B. The strings. She worked for Amanda.

In his business, a part of his life—Amanda who already tied him to too many things he'd prefer to let go.

Definitely not the kind of hassle he needed.

He shook his head and caught a glimpse of motion from the corner of his eye as Cali pushed through the revolving doors and stepped out into the fresh morning air. A gentle breeze caught a few auburn curls that had slipped free of their tie, framing her face in a soft show of light, color and motion.

His chest tightened, his groin quickly following suit.

Hell.

Didn't matter. She looked good. There was some chemistry. So what?

The big head was in control and it was telling him to ignore the little head's apparent unflagging interest. He wouldn't give in to the persistent itch that had him speculating as to what it would take to get Cali beneath him, because, logically, he knew he was better off keeping things hands-off.

The only place he had to get Cali was into her apartment.

Jumping out of the car, Jake rounded to the passenger side to help her in. "All set?"

"Yes, thanks." She settled back, reaching for the seatbelt over her shoulder. The fabric of her top pulled taut with the twist of her body. She crossed to fasten the belt, and the swell of one creamy breast pushed forward as the deep vee of her halter offered a tantalizing view into the shadowy hollow of her cleavage. A rush of blood straight to Jake's head was followed immediately by its plummet south, to the usurper beneath his belt.

Oh, now, that was ridiculous. He was a doctor. A heart surgeon. He saw enough breasts and cleavage on a daily basis that to be affected by a peek down a gorgeous woman's shirt was ludicrous. He swung the door closed and shook out the fingers that had locked around it.

Enough was enough. She was a woman. He handled women with ease.

Returning to his seat, he forced a casual tone. "Do you mind the top down?"

Cali shook her head then smiled up at the Chicago sky, bright with only a few cottonball clouds strewn above the lake. "Not at all. Days like today are the reason convertibles were created."

"Couldn't agree with you more." He grinned, shifted into gear, and pulled into the traffic headed for the Drive.

Beneath the sun's warm rays, sandy beaches alternated with rocky shores and grassy stretches of park as they sped north along the lakefront. New buildings with their shining glass and metal knifed up into the vast blue sky, while the blunt stone façades of monuments to old Chicago endured beside them in classic countenance.

Quiet, Cali watched the passing terrain, fidgeting with her fingers. This was crazy. They were both stiff and overly polite, and after last night there was no excuse for it. They'd talked and laughed for hours without a moment's awkward pause. So they weren't going to pursue a physical relationship? So what? That didn't mean they couldn't enjoy the platonic elements of their connection. Today circumstance had thrown them together again, and he, for one, was going to make the most of it.

Jake glanced over at her and, keeping one hand on the wheel, he caught hers with the other. "Cali, I'm the same guy from last night. We had a great time together. It was *fun*. We've agreed sex is a mistake, but we're both adults. Let's just relax about it."

She shifted in her seat, angling toward him. Her gaze touched on his mouth for a moment, and he knew she was remembering the way they'd kissed, but then she met his eyes and her oh-so-serious expression softened into something closer to what it had been the night before.

"You're right. Last night was so easy, and this morning…." She shook her head, as if wishing she could forget it. "So, friends?"

"Yeah, why not? Friends." *Friends who didn't have sex*, he thought, moving his hand back to the wheel. Even if they did have an arsenal of mind-blowing, explosive kisses behind them. The devil in him flashed her a wink. "Friends with a past."

She arched a brow at him. "A past?"

"Yeah, something to laugh about so it doesn't become some uncomfortable, unspeakable, taboo subject everyone dances around and gets all embarrassed about."

"Oh, *that* kind of friends with a past," she answered, her smile spreading. "Sure. Now I get it."

"All we need to do is make some kind of joke about it, and we'll be back on track."

She was quiet for a moment, though the silence wasn't strained or uncomfortable this time. Then she ran her fingers over the black leather interior of the Mercedes. "So, you pick up all your dates in the back halls of bars?"

Jake barked out a laugh and settled deeper into his seat. "This coming from you? Phone booth?"

"Oh, please." She flicked her hand dismissively as her lips stretched into that smile he couldn't stop working for. "I was dragged there."

"Carried. I'm too smooth to drag anyone anywhere. It was romantic."

"Not." Cali snickered. "It was dirty. The good kind. Fun. But definitely dirty."

Definitely fun. "Does that mean I get a page in your dirty little secrets book?"

"More like a footnote as a once-in-a-lifetime exception to the rule."

Jake grinned. This was the woman from last night. Fun. Cool.

Friends worked for him. No strings. No mess. No complications. His head was in the right place about it. Now his body just had to get with the program.

Ten minutes later, the elevator doors opened to the seventeenth floor of the Lincoln Park building Cali would be calling home for the next two months. She followed a step behind as they walked to the door marked "17D". Jake dug into the pocket of his jeans, retrieved a set of keys on a small ring, and flipped them out into his wide palm. "You've got three keys. Your apartment door, your mailbox, and this large one is for the gym down on thirteen. It's open twenty-four hours, so if you get the urge to work off some tension after a long day of espionage it's available. Parking is on three, and your apartment has a space assigned in case you have a visitor." He raised an eyebrow. "You know anyone in town here?"

It was a simple question, but suddenly Cali felt the possessive undercurrent beneath it and tensed. "No. This move is all about work. Just as well I don't know anyone."

"Aside from me that is."

"Sure." She smiled feebly, knowing that, friends or not, she didn't really have time for him either. "Aside from you."

Jake unlocked the door and then swung it open, standing aside for Cali to enter. "Amanda says this project she's got you on is a pretty big deal. She's got a lot of respect for your skills."

Cali beamed. "Thanks, I'm really excited." Then, taking several steps inside, she gasped. "This is incredible." The apartment was spacious, with high ceilings and a glorious bank of windows overlooking the lakefront below. She craned to see down the long hall to the right, before spinning back to check out the kitchen and the fireplace. "My sublets are usually half this size and facing a brick wall."

Jake folded his arms across his chest, his stance wide. "I don't think all the Chicago operatives score a sweet pad like this, but apparently there was some problem with the agency Amanda normally uses for temporary housing. This place was available, so…. I'm glad you like it."

"It's gorgeous."

"I agree." His eyes were on her, moving slowly over her face, her body, and suddenly the vast apartment closed in. Then, just as quickly, his gaze shuttered and shifted to the windows as he crossed the open room to get a better look. "You've got a great view out here. The water, the Drive."

The muscles across his back flexed as he raised a hand to push long fingers through his hair. Hair she'd had *her* fingers wound in the night before—

What was she doing, watching the way he moved when she'd just agreed to this friends-with-a-past business? It had sounded like a great deal—until the apartment door closed behind them and once again they were alone.

Alone was bad. Eyeballing Jake was worse.

He turned from the window and caught her staring. Whatever it was he'd been planning to say was forgotten as his gaze intensified, heated.

She needed to look away. Get him out of her apartment, out of her space, out of eyeballing distance for sure—but she didn't move. Couldn't break the visual contact that seemed to be holding her captive. Her panic rose as she scoured a suddenly vacant mind for anything to say. "Well, thank you for bringing me over. I should start getting settled."

"Your things haven't been delivered yet," he said, his gaze dropping to her mouth, sending her thoughts straight to his kiss and the masculine, seductive taste of him.

No. This was Amanda's Jackson.

He needed to go.

"Mmm-hmm, right. But I can think about where I want things…once they get here."

Those blue eyes darkened as if a storm was moving in behind them. He took a step in her direction and her lungs constricted.

"Wha—what are you doing?" she stammered, taking a halting step back.

"You know what I'm doing," he answered without pretense, matching her retreat with one long-legged stride.

"We—we're friends. Friends with a past, remember?"

"I've reconsidered. Friends isn't going to work. Not for us."

"Why not?"

His left hand caught her around the waist. "Friends don't look at friends the way you're looking at me."

"It was an accident! I was thinking about last night for one second," she said, her voice rising with her panic. "But I'm done now. Over it. Really ready to move from the past to the present."

Jake nodded, satisfaction evident in the smug curve of his smile. "Me too."

She put her arms up to stop him, but they buckled against the crush of his chest as he leaned in to her with a soft, sinking brush of his lips against hers. Somewhere between a taste and caress, the slow stroke of his kiss blanked her mind of anything beyond the gentle suction against her mouth and the stirring need low in her belly.

Her nipples peaked, her body begged to curve into his, but her mind knew better. She had plans. She couldn't follow her heart or trust the instinct that told her to wrap her arms tight around this man's neck and hold on.

No! Wrenching away from the kiss, Cali shut her eyes against the temptation of his gaze. "Damn it, Jake! We agreed this was a mistake."

Jake hadn't moved; his arms still held her. She forced herself to look up at him.

"It doesn't feel like a mistake. It didn't last night either." His head bowed so that his lips grazed the outer ridge of her ear. "Do you know how hard it was to let you go? How much I wanted to follow you?"

His arms circled tighter, holding her against him in a way that warmed her from the inside out.

Thank God he hadn't followed. She wouldn't have been able to resist, and then everything today would have been that much worse. She closed her eyes. As if it wasn't bad enough already.

She'd been breaking her rules since the minute he'd sat down beside her at the bar. Begging for an excuse to sidestep the careful plans she'd laid. And now, what if Amanda found out? She had a second chance at her career and she couldn't blow it on some feel-good fantasy. "That was last night. When I thought it was *only* last night." When she'd thought Jake nothing more than a few moments' indiscretion, free and clear of ties to her work or future.

The muscles surrounding her tensed, as though her admission somehow bothered him. Well, too bad.

Jake let her go and stepped back a pace. "Cali, I see the way you're looking at me—"

She cut him off with a slash of her hand. There was no room for pride here. "I don't get out much, okay? You're an attractive guy and I'm not immune. But that doesn't change the fact that I have priorities higher than my libido."

Finally some straight thinking she could feel good about, even if the look of frustrated aggravation on Jake's face was something she couldn't. He studied her from beneath the grim set of his brow and then nodded. "I get the priorities, and I already told you I wasn't looking for something serious—believe me, I'm not—but this attraction. It's intense. You think you can just ignore it?"

She bit down on her lips, drew her arms across her chest.

She had to. He was a risk on too many levels. Because of Amanda's feelings. Because of her own. He was a risk she wouldn't take. "I can and will. I'm sorry, Jake. Starting tomorrow I'll barely have time for a glass of water, let alone getting swept up in whatever chemistry there is between us. Trust me, that's just how these assignments go. We probably won't even see each other again while I'm here."

Stuffing his hands into his pockets, he cocked his head. "So, out of sight, out of mind, then?"

"Yes." The ache in her chest would be gone as soon as he left. It would work. She just needed him to go. To vanish into the city and let her focus on her goal.

"Okay. Good luck with the project." Jake smiled that easy smile at her, hoarding all the confidence in the room as he offered a no-hard-feelings wave.

"Thank you."

He stopped, as if struck by a thought, and turned back. "If you have any problems or questions, just knock next door. 17E."

"Who lives there?" she asked as she went for her purse to jot down the name.

"I do. It's my building. Take it easy, neighbor." He grinned and walked out.

Her purse clattered to floor at her feet as Jake shut the door behind him, his low chuckle cut off by the latch.

CHAPTER SIX

IT WAS Wednesday, and dusk had fallen as Cali jostled her laptop and messenger-style briefcase, pushing backward through the swinging door into the fluorescent lit convenience Mecca known as the Snappy Convenience Store. Bells rang above her head, announcing her entrance.

"Amanda, hold on one sec." Phone pinched between shoulder and ear, she snagged a plastic basket from the stack and descended into the third aisle.

Her boss groaned through the line. "Good Lord, what are you doing?"

"Sorry, sorry," she answered, moving by rote toward the international snacks. "Just picking up some supplies. Okay, so I've looked into the discrepancy we picked up this morning. The numbers are off—I know that much. But what kind of delay we're facing I won't be able to tell you until I've met with Reynolds to get a better understanding."

"He should be arriving back from Atlanta this evening, and I've left messages in addition to yours. Keep me in the loop on this one."

"Will do." Cali stifled a yawn.

A quiet laugh filtered through the line. "You sound ready to drop. Have you gotten all moved in at home?"

"Ah, I wish." At the sound of the doorbells clanging, Cali shot a quick glance to the front of the store and stopped short, her breath leaking out in a slow hiss. Jake Tyler strode in and, shirt collar open, cuffs rolled, offered a warm greeting to the clerk behind the register. Distracted, Cali made her way deeper into the aisle, shoulders hunched in an attempt to avoid his notice. For days she'd been unsuccessfully trying to dodge Jake. She'd peek out into the hall to make sure he wasn't there, only to cross his path twenty minutes later, running at the lakefront. Hustle through the lobby to catch a closing elevator, only to find him standing at the security desk, ready to throw some frustratingly engaging line her way that had her laughing before she could think to stop. Escaping the flash of that cocky grin was proving to be an exercise in futility. Though one she couldn't quite regret. He was *fun*.

"Hello?" Amanda's voice through the line pulled her back to the now. Her job, her boss. Even when he wasn't trying Jake got in the way. "You wish what?"

"There was some mix-up," she answered quietly. "Half my things ended up in Washington. I'm supposed to be getting them this weekend, but it's been a long week so far."

"What are you missing?"

"The furniture all came, which was great." She knelt, flipping through the assortment of cellophane-packaged dry snacks. "But whatever went into a box didn't. So pretty much…well, everything."

"Wait—you don't have dishes? Cooking equipment? Clothing?"

There wasn't much to do about it. The truck was in another state. "I bought some new clothes and a few essentials."

"Did you tell Jackson? He could help you out with some supplies. He could help with anything you need while you're there. The man has a million skills."

Yeah, like kissing, and long, intimate conversation. Cali closed her eyes, hating this feeling that she was betraying her boss, a woman who had given her the break—a second chance to prove herself—that no one else would grant. "Uh, I haven't seen much of Jake." Peeking around the corner, she let out a relieved breath to see him pulling a few bills from his front pocket for what looked like a current affairs magazine. Almost done. "Honestly, don't worry about it, Amanda. I'm not the first person in history to spend a week surviving on microwave meals and plastic forks. It's as good an excuse to skip cooking as you can get."

"Ever the optimist, huh?"

Cali rolled her eyes, thinking about the blue streak she'd cursed that very morning when faced with the single pair of heels she'd brought. "That's me."

Papers shuffled in the background and Amanda's voice returned, sharp and professional. "Okay, well, hang in there and get back to me on the timetable when you have something."

"Will do, Amanda. You can count on me." Cali disconnected the call and reached back to tuck her phone into her pocket. The bags slung awkwardly around her shoulders slipped forward, the shifting weight pulling Cali to her knees with a muffled grunt. Scrunching her eyes closed, she forced a calming breath before snatching a pouch of Japanese trail mix from the rack and dropping it into her basket.

Dinner.

Even a microwave meal was too labor-intensive after the day she'd had.

Pushing back to a crouch, Cali moved to stand—only to find herself lifted to her feet. With a gasp, she spun. "Jake!"

"Krissy up front thought someone was crawling around back here. What are you doing on the floor?"

She blinked, feeling the hot lick of humiliation in her cheeks. "No—but—I wasn't crawling—"

He chuckled, waving her away as he smoothly stripped her of the heavy briefcase. "Just weighted down by your cargo, huh?"

Nodding, she reached to reclaim her bag. "Yes, but you don't have to carry that for me."

He raised a brow at her, and she had to acknowledge how much better she felt without the weight of the overloaded bag. "Well, thank you."

"Welcome. We'll walk back together."

Jake took a step forward, but Cali found herself rooted to her spot. Her limbs unwilling to follow.

"Jake—"

He turned, noting her stagnated progress with a downward pull to his mouth. "Take it easy, Cali. I'm just carrying your bag."

"I know." And yet her feet refused to move.

"So what's the problem?" He watched her, awareness glinting in his eyes. "Unless you don't trust yourself in the elevator with me." His brow was raised in subtle challenge and she had to look away, unwilling to acknowledge her fear of being trapped together for seventeen floors in a tiny box that took her mind straight back to a phone booth flooded with jazz and need. An unwelcome wave of heat washed through her belly, frustrating her to the point where she had to clench her fists before daring another look at the man who spurred such intense reactions.

She shook her head.

"I think I'm going to grab a few more things, since I'm already here. Why don't you go ahead?"

After a beat, Jake handed her briefcase back, slipping the strap over her shoulder and straightening her jacket. "Whatever you want, Cali."

The weight of the bag dug into her strained muscle, but she smiled as though it were nothing.

Watching him leave, Cali dropped a few random selections from the shelves into her basket. When he was safely out of the store, she walked to the front counter to make her purchases. Through the plate glass window she could see Jake halfway down the block, drawing to a stop when a pretty blonde crossed the traffic with a broad smile and an eager wave to get to him. A baseless, utterly irrational stab of jealousy cut through her at seeing his arm slip across the woman's shoulders.

A familiar ping alerted her to a waiting text. Absently she plucked out the phone and read the message. Reynolds was back and could meet with her now. Perfect. Cali pushed out a steady breath and sent a short reply that she'd meet him in twenty minutes, back in conference room four.

This was why she'd come to Chicago. Not for the attention of some sexy man who couldn't walk down the street without a beautiful woman throwing herself into his path. But, even so, she couldn't fight one last glance down the street.

Three hours later, Cali made it home. The news from Reynolds wasn't what she'd wanted to hear, but at least she knew what she was up against. Tomorrow morning she'd wrestle the project back on track.

Dropping her bags in a heap by the door, she kicked off her shoes and groaned as blood surged to her aching toes. Eyes closed, she dropped onto the couch and dragged the unopened bag of trail mix up to her chest—fairly certain she was still hungry, but beyond the point where she could differentiate one discomfort from the next. She'd forgotten her bottled water by the door. Cranking her head to the side, she debated exerting the energy to get it. Her gaze drifted from the flimsy Snappy Store bag to a white piece of paper on the floor a foot over. A note? Had the movers been by? There hadn't been any messages on her phone.

She forced herself from the comforting hold of the cushions and swept it up.

No, not the movers. Jake.

"Stop by my apartment when you get home tonight."

"Tonight" was underlined. He owned the building—maybe he'd spoken to the movers. Thinking back to the blonde, she wondered if he'd have company. He wouldn't have left the note if he wasn't alone. Would he? Only one way to find out.

Shoulders back, head high, stomach in knots, she strode down the hall to Jake's door and knocked. Waited. Maybe he wouldn't answer and she'd be able to skulk back to her apartment without having to face him.

No luck.

Within seconds, the lock sounded and her fate was sealed. The door swung open and rock music spilled out into the hall.

"Cali?" Jake, bare chest glistening with sweat, dark hair pushed back in damp disarray, rested his forearm against the door frame and scanned the length of her. "You okay? You don't look so good."

Her mouth went dry, her head light. Hell, *she* might not look so good, but she'd never seen anything as criminally attractive as Jake in her entire life.

It was obscene. He should know better than to answer the door like that. Sure, he wasn't naked. The longish black basketball shorts hung low on his trim hips covered a stretch of him, but she couldn't keep her eyes from trailing down the crisp hair of his abdomen to—

"Cali," he growled, "eyes up here, if you don't mind." Her

gaze, filled with horrified embarrassment, collided with the pure masculine amusement of his. "I'm guessing your awed silence has something to do with that 'man-candy' thing you mentioned the other morning?"

Okay, that did the trick and broke through her haze of lust. She coughed out a laugh. "Get over yourself."

He raised a brow at her. "It's not like *I* was gawking. At least your color's back. You were looking a little pale there."

"I wasn't gawking!" she protested, waiting for a bolt of lightning to strike her down for the lie. "You just took me by surprise opening the door like…" she flapped her hand around at his body "…like that! Jeez, what if there were children out here?"

"Hey, it's almost twelve on a school night. Kids out this late wouldn't be up to much good anyway." He grinned. "I couldn't take credit for corrupting them."

"I didn't realize— I didn't think—" She'd come knocking on his door at midnight. Shame-faced, she focused on a point halfway down the hall. This was *so* sending the wrong message. Finally, she held up the note. "I didn't realize it was so late. I had to go back to work, so I only just got this."

Jake shifted in her peripheral vision. "Don't worry about the time. I was kind of keyed up from a case today and was working it off. I'm glad you came over." He stepped back. "Come on in for a minute."

"No," she nearly choked. She didn't have to look to know that sinful smile played on his lips. "No, thank you. I just—"

"Cali, I'm standing in the doorway, dripping sweat on the hall carpet. Come in a minute and let me clean up. I've got some stuff for you."

She didn't want to go into his apartment. If ninety seconds in an elevator seemed bad to her, there was no way she could brace herself against this half-naked-behind-closed-doors business.

"Inside, Cali." He leaned out and reached for her hand. "Think of the children."

"Oh, fine." Rolling her eyes, she brushed his hand away and nudged past him into the apartment, surprised to find the space was significantly larger than hers and filled with an eclectic mix of styles that combined to create a cool setting epitomizing Jake.

An enormous oriental rug covering much of the hardwood floor somehow complemented the modern blown-glass light fixtures, and tribal art hung on the walls. It would have been sophisticated styling if not for the treadmill parked in front of a sixty-five-inch flatscreen television scrolling financial stats.

Jake walked over to the stereo and turned the music down, then grabbed a small towel and carelessly dragged it over his face, neck and torso.

Deep breaths.

"Okay, Cali." The playful glint was gone from his eyes. "Amanda told me your stuff hasn't been delivered yet. You should have come over."

She might have—only every time she got within a few feet of this man she found herself giving in to a pull she had to deny. "I was fine. If I'd really needed anything I would have knocked or just gone and gotten it."

He stared at her then, those blue eyes holding her in place, making her squirm, challenging her as if he doubted what she'd said.

To hell with him. "I would have."

"Sure—that's why you've been eating microwave meals off plastic forks all week."

Amanda.

Rather than get into it any further, Cali stepped over the cardboard box atop the low coffee table. There were two plates, a skillet, two settings of silverware, a roll of paper towels, a pot, a four-cup coffee-maker, a mug from some pharmaceutical company and two glasses packed with a dish towel and a potholder. Her throat tightened at the thoughtful generosity of this man she was working so hard to avoid. "Thank you."

"No big deal."

She shook her head, daring a glance at him. "It is to me."

Jake offered a nod, watching her with eyes that saw more than she wanted to reveal. Eyes that echoed the satisfaction curving through his lips at whatever he'd found. "So I guess I'm your hero, then?"

She swallowed, unable to look away, barely able to speak. "God, your ego."

That smug smile pulled to one side and he closed the distance between them in two lazy strides. Her heart slammed against her chest as he leaned closer, until his breath warmed the whorl of her ear and the heat of his body licked across the scant space between them. "Yeah, well, stop stroking it and maybe it'll go away."

Her traitorous body seized under the rough stroke of his voice and she stumbled back, shocked at the ease with which he could get past her defenses. She cast him a sidelong glance, afraid of what he'd manage if she let him out of her sight for too long.

Jake tossed the towel toward the treadmill, where it caught over one of the rails, and turned back to flash a wide grin. "Come on. I'll carry this box back to your place and then let you get some rest."

CHAPTER SEVEN

BY SATURDAY morning the bulk of the MetroTrek delay had been resolved, but Cali was suffering. She'd worked until nearly two a.m., only to be awoken four hours later with a phone call from the movers. An hour and a half later, twenty-two boxes had been delivered. By nine, the pressure in her head—a slow, radiating throb behind her eyes—was enough to make any sane person curl up into a ball on the floor of a dark closet.

But Cali wasn't sane. She was a week behind schedule on getting her living space in order, and now that her belongings had finally arrived no amount of sleep deprivation was going to keep her from it. As with everything else even remotely tied to this stint in Chicago, she'd found herself off track and out of sync with a plan she'd lived by for the last three years. She simply couldn't stomach the idea of letting it go for even one minute longer. So, exhausted, she hung up her clothes, put the linens away, and now was up to her elbows in an eruption of newsprint and bubble wrap.

Shifting her weight from her groaning knees, she rolled onto the balls of her feet into a crouch, wiped at her forehead with the back of an ink-darkened hand and glanced out over the lake-front and the waves glinting in the late-morning light below.

She should have felt good about her progress, only the

slow-going drag and monotony of her task was weighing on her as never before. It didn't make sense. This was the routine. It worked. So why the restlessness?

Gathering an armful of packing paper, she folded the mess into a recyclable bag. She'd break to dump the trash, stretch out her limbs, and then get back at it.

The lobby doors were propped open, allowing for a hint of the day's fresh, early-summer air and sunshine to circulate within the otherwise dark lobby. Jake strode through the open doors, following the parquet past the iron-railed stairwell toward the elevator. Catching the doors as they were sliding closed, he stepped into the car to find Cali—an adorably dirty Cali—peering up at him. He stopped short. Dark smudges streaked her skin from cheek to chin and ear to brow, and her auburn curls sprang in wild disarray.

"Wait, don't tell me. Mud-wrestling—and what happened to my VIP pass?"

Even her answering laugh sounded exhausted, but her smile was genuine as she wearily answered. "Hi, Jake. My stuff came this morning."

"My second guess. That's great. How's the unpacking going?"

Her head tilted back against the corner of the car, exposing the slender length of her neck. "About half done. Maybe a little more." She blew out a breath. "I just can't wait to finish. I'm ready to be settled in, you know."

"Yep. I get that." He remembered the frustration of a life in limbo all too clearly, and imagined that with the frequency Cali moved the stability of a home environment was even more important to her.

As she rested against the wall, the thumb she'd hooked into her front pocket slipped free, and she jerked as if she'd been three-quarters to sleep already. Jake's focus narrowed on the smudges around her face, the shadows beneath her eyes. "Did you sleep?"

"A little. Late-night working."

He reached out and brushed a streak of dirt from her cheek-bone, letting his thumb run slowly across the delicate rise. No reaction beyond the sluggish shifting of her gaze to meet his. This was beyond tired. "That's it. As a professional courtesy to the ER doctors on duty today, I'm taking you off box-cutting duty before you take off a digit."

Her nose crinkled in confusion.

"I'm going to help you," he clarified, in his most un-yielding tone.

She was beat, all right, without any fight left to muster. Too tired to shield the relief and gratitude that flooded her eyes. Too tired to make up some lame excuse to try and keep her distance. "Really?"

Jake nodded as the elevator doors opened on seventeen. He took her arm, leading her down the hall to his door. "Quick pitstop here for some emergency rations."

Letting her in to his place, he went straight for the fridge and grabbed a couple of cans of soda. "Caffeine boost," he said, handing her one. "Drink up."

Cali tipped the can back, taking a long swallow, and then followed him down the hall.

"Jake, you've got to have more exciting things to do than sit around and unload boxes with me."

As a rule, most anything was more exciting than unpacking someone else's stuff. Except this someone was Cali—and she happened to have a four-inch smudge of dirt peaking out of her cleavage. But even without that tantalizing attraction he liked being around her. Liked getting a rise out her and watching her frantic retreat when he got just that much too close.

"I don't know. I could get lucky and score the box with your racy panty collection and your dirty tell-all diary."

A reluctant smile spread over her lips as one fist settled on her hip. "Hate to rain on your parade, but neither exists."

"Then I'll just have to settle for this being my good deed for the day."

"By keeping me out of the emergency room?"

"Like you'd even make it there. One glimpse of the blood and you'd be out on the floor, your A-positive staining the hardwood. Really, my generosity is selfishly motivated."

She snickered behind him, sounding more alert already. "The cleaning and all?"

"Exactly. Now, let's get a move on."

Within a few hours they'd finished unpacking, and Cali's apartment had begun to look like a home. Pictures of her family sat out on a corner table, books and knick-knacks filled her shelves. They'd even hung a few black and white framed prints on the walls. She'd tried to shoo him out over those hours, but Jake wouldn't give and they'd ended up working and talking through the early afternoon.

It had been easy. Fun.

Being with Cali was unlike being with anyone else. There was just something about her he couldn't quite get enough of. She'd asked him about his marriage and, to his surprise, he'd actually told her. Given her the nutshell version of his biggest failure. The "high school sweethearts getting hitched too early" song and dance. He'd been able to own up to the fact that he hadn't had the slightest clue as to how to be a good husband, and Cali had seemed to understand.

When she'd asked what had finally happened to end things, he'd told her about Pam's affair in one concise sentence. He didn't like to talk about it, didn't like to think about it, but for some reason he'd been as close to revealing the details to Cali as he'd ever gotten with anyone. There was just something about her that made him curious, made him want to talk—made him want more than that. If he examined it long enough, he imagined that that *something* had a lot to do with the fact that she was a temporary attraction in his life. Nothing quite as safe as a woman who couldn't even commit herself to a single city, let alone one man, and would most likely be living across the ocean within a few months' time. He didn't have to trust her for life, just a few weeks or so. No time for failed expectations or betrayals. No time for anything to get deep enough to regret. He could relax around her, and it felt good.

Now the dishes had been run through the washer, and they stood in the kitchen, emptying the racks. The last leg.

Jake pulled out four slender stemmed glasses, still warm from the heat cycle, then slid them into the ironwork rack suspended above the sink. There were a few circular slots reserved for wine bottles. He'd bring over a Santa Margarita he had at his place, and maybe a Fiddlehead too.

Behind him, Cali was muttering to herself about the shelves. "Salad and dinner plates. Bowls…."

He grabbed a stack of plates and handed them over, falling into the easy rhythm of working side by side with her as naturally as breathing.

"Thanks. I love getting this stuff put away."

"It looks good in here," he said, nodding to the half-filled cabinets. Then, taking in the dark circles under her eyes—the ones that hadn't washed off when he'd brought a damp cloth out for her—he added, "Cali, you need some rest."

"I'm too excited to rest." Then she smiled at him. "So, you know you really *are* my hero, don't you?"

The things she did to his ego. "Finally—some recognition."

"We're done after this one." Shaking her head with a laugh, she grabbed the last item from the dishwasher. Jake slid the empty racks in, then closed the door, sharing her sense of completion. Leaning a hip against the sink, he turned to her, surprised by the peaceful satisfaction in watching the line of her body extend to house the last dish.

It was nice—only suddenly it wasn't.

His mouth drew down as he recognized the familiar sense of companionable domesticity for what it was. His gut tensed as he tried to ignore the niggling unease settling over him. It was five minutes and didn't mean anything. Probably nothing more than some kind of emotional muscle memory, wired to sharing space in a kitchen. Nothing a little reprogramming couldn't handle. Some whipped cream, ripe berries and two days of sweaty sex against every available surface and he'd be able to unload the dishwasher without getting caught up in some rubbish warm, fuzzy contentment trap. Mental note to get on that—ASAP.

"I need to get a step-stool in here." Cali went onto her toes with a serving plate in hand.

Perfect. He focused on the sweet, heart-shaped curve of her bottom, letting his gaze linger at that vee between her legs before moving up to the sexy stretch of bare skin between the hem of a tee-shirt that clung to her curves and the top of her jeans.

Playtime was over. *This* was what he wanted.

"I've got it." Jake's voice was closer than she'd expected. She turned to find him right behind her. He set one hand at her waist, crowding her, as he took the platter from her grasp and, reaching over her, stowed it in the uppermost cabinet.

Her fingers gripped the countertop at either side of her hips as Jake lowered his deep blue gaze to hers, smiling that lazy, smooth smile.

This man had the most beautiful mouth she'd ever seen. And she didn't have to imagine or guess what those firm, chiseled lips would feel like rubbing against her own. She already knew. Ecstasy.

Flashes of the phone booth came in quick succession as her back pressed into the counter behind her and her torso absorbed the heat of Jake's body.

Oh, God, she could barely breathe.

His chest was right there, and he smelled so good, and her mouth was suddenly dry. She tried to conjure Amanda, hoping the mental image of her boss getting all breathy about *Jackson* would be enough to douse the flames licking low in her belly—get her to stop this mind-traveling back to that night in the bar.

Slow jazz. The seductive, gliding caress of his tongue against hers. His ragged groan, "Tell me to stop."

Only it didn't work. She was alone in her apartment with Amanda's Jackson, standing there watching him tempt her into seeing him as just Jake. The truth was he'd been tempting her all day. Longer, even.

He *was* just Jake. He'd been with her all day. Making her laugh. Making her think. Talking about life and—and she was making a mistake letting herself think that way for even a second. Only she couldn't stop.

A shiver ran the length of her spine, skirting around to tighten the skin across her chest, hitching her breath to a halt. There was no stopping it, this desire that built within her every minute they were together, that jumped and flared at every innocuous touch. He read it in her eyes. He had to. She needed him to.

His pupils dilated, roiled with turbulent emotion. He was going to kiss her, and this time—

"Turn around and lean forward over the counter."

"Wh-what?" Cali's eyes flared wide, but Jake took her by the shoulders and steadily turned her away from him. Her heart slammed a staccato beat against her ribs. She couldn't move, couldn't voice a word of protest as his wide, strong hand spanned her lower back, then skimmed up her spine, using a gentle but firm pressure to bend her over.

He gathered the hair that hung heavy down her back, parted it at her nape and, twisting the untamed curls, pushed them to fall forward over her shoulders. And then those long fingers were sifting through the weighty mass, tugging at the strands so tiny sparks of pleasure flared at the roots. The tingling sensation of shifting follicles had her fighting a groan, only to lose the battle when his hands moved with steady pressure in a downward stroke from the base of her skull across the slope of her shoulders.

"Jake," she gasped as his thumbs pressed into the taut tissues astride her spine, circling slowly until her worn muscles succumbed, releasing their tension to his ministrations.

He worked the muscle groups, large and small, his every touch and murmured comment—"Hard? Like that?"—melting her resolve.

Making her want more.

Need more.

Warm breath bathed the exposed skin of her neck as he worked the joints of her shoulders, her upper arms, traps and deltoids. His fingers walked the path of delicate bones that collared her neck. Touched on the tops of her pectoral muscles, making her breasts peak and ache for the attention that remained just out of reach. Dipped lower in an elusive caress, still inches from her nipples, before retreating to the spread of her shoulders.

His skilled hands followed around her ribs, moving over her in confident, deliberate strokes. Easing lower. Locking around her hips as he kneaded the small of her back.

"You're so tight."

Cali's teeth sank into her bottom lip at the gruff sound of his provocative words—words that conjured erotic images— used in a context to torment her.

"You like that?"

Her belly knotted as her body went liquid beneath his touch.

"Jake," she gasped again, his name riding a quivering breath. "Please...."

The heat of him radiated over her, so close, but not quite touching.

"Tell me what you want, Cali." His voice was rough velvet at her ear, making her knees weak. Her body burn. "Tell me. And I'll give it to you."

She was lost. Her mind spun, trying to grasp onto a solid reason she shouldn't, but there was nothing beyond this aching need. No sense. No reason. No more resistance.

"Please...touch me."

"Like this, Cali?"

And then the distance between them was gone as all that warmth was coupled with solid muscle and man. His mouth closed over the base of her neck and his hands snaked around her belly, slipping beneath the hem of her tee-shirt to cup the swells of her tender breasts.

An answering moan was all she could manage as the fingers of one of his hands curled into the top of her bra. He caught her beaded nipple between his knuckles and squeezed gently.

"Or like this?" he asked, scraping his teeth over the muscle at her shoulder.

Her knees buckled under the sensual assault. Jake's gruff, sexy laughter rasped against her spine as he held her to him.

"Too much, sweetheart?" he asked with mock concern as he teased a hot palm across the skin of her belly. "Should I stop?"

"Don't." Reaching over her head, she sifted her fingers into the dark silk of his hair, holding him close to her. "Don't stop. I can't stop—"

The shrill ring of her phone sounded from the counter in front of her, shocking her frayed nerves.

"No," she groaned. Her body, enslaved by a touch she'd been too long denied, vibrated with need.

She'd stilled in Jake's arms, but his sensual assault continued. His hands ran from her breasts to her thighs, pressing her into the hold of his hard body. "Who is it?" he murmured at her ear.

A glance at the display showed the name and number. "IT guy working this weekend… He's getting back to me on overtime projections… It's going to be quick…but I—I…." Jake sucked the fleshy lobe of her ear into his mouth. "I— mmmm…."

His hands skimmed up her body, following the line of her raised arms until he had both her hands held in his. Pressing one into the counter in front of her, he slid his thick fingers between hers, holding her in place.

The other hand he guided to wrap across her waist, settling in a loose hold at her hip. "Don't take it." Gentle suction pulled at the nape of her neck followed by the light rasp of teeth.

She'd been waiting on the information. It wasn't a huge deal, but this employee was giving up part of his weekend because of her mandate. He wouldn't leave until she'd spoken to him. Disappointment washed through her, twisting her stomach with frustration so intense it hurt. Ignoring the call wasn't an option. But after—

Freeing the hand at her hip, she grasped for the phone and connected. Put it to her ear. "Calista McGovern."

On the other end of the line the IT guy began rambling about numbers and his projections. Cali closed her eyes and focused on the metallic voice as Jake's palm slid hot across her belly. His body, broad and powerful, against her back.

"Thank you. That's what I was looking for." Drawing on every brain cell she could muster, she forced the words from her lips in what she prayed was coherent order. This call couldn't end fast enough. "Send me the file and we'll be set."

Hot breath, and the sense of a smile behind it, whispered at her other ear. "You sound breathless, Cali… Concentrate for me."

Jake's fingers splayed wide, tugging her closer into him. His breath was moist and warm, loosing undeniable chemical reactions to snake through her system, justifications to lick at all the tender, needy places, driving her blind with desire.

The call would only take a minute. His touch felt so good. She could handle it.

"God, you're making me hot. You need to end this call, because I can't not touch you," he growled. "Can you feel me? Feel what you do to me?"

Yes. She could feel him—his steely length was pressing against her.

A single nod.

Answered with a cool lick at the shell of her ear, turning her body to liquid fire.

More details about some unexpected delays in her right ear. *Please!*

"Does that make you hot—to know what you do to me?" The question, punctuated by a nip at her left ear, made her body seize. "Does it make you wet?"

"Mmm-hmm," she answered both men, her need ratcheting higher by the second. This was insanity, and yet she couldn't summon the strength to pull away.

Jake slipped his fingers free of the hand he'd pinned to the counter. Then he began to run both his palms over her breasts in slow, tight circles that had her pushing into his hands, her head dropping back against his shoulder and her eyes drifting closed.

"I don't know if you're talking to me or your IT guy. I'm going to have to find out for myself."

Her eyes flew open as his hand brushed over the fly of her jeans, opening the snap and the zipper. He wouldn't.... But then his knee nudged between her thighs to widen her stance as his fingers skimmed at the sensitive skin below her navel.

And she knew—

He dipped into her panties as the IT guy droned on about the working conditions at his last job. Wait—she hadn't followed the transition of the conversation. What else had she missed?

Her body tensed, but not from pleasure. She'd gotten in so far over her head the room spun. This was a disaster!

Except that thick fingers were slipping against her aching wetness, parting and pushing into her. Her mouth opened in a silent cry as her body betrayed her, seizing in an attempt to draw him deeper. Jake was at her ear again, hot and urgent.

"Time to hang up, Cali. You'll call him back."

He moved in and out of her, so good, so deep.

"Cali?" He stilled.

Only her body didn't care that the thrust and retreat had ceased. The penetration had pushed her past the edge of control. She was falling.

"Hang up, sweetheart."

And then the phone was out of her hand, abruptly disconnected. She cried out her completion in gasping breaths, with Jake's midnight voice at her ear, talking her through the crashing waves of an orgasm so strong it had battered her senses and convictions into the dust to get free.

"Cali?" Jake turned her around, tucking her into the hold of his arms. She peered up at him as the cool, wet path of shame streaked down her cheek.

Her throat was too tight to speak so she shook her head.

"Don't look like that." He caught one guilty tear with his thumb, tried to brush it away. "Sweetheart, it's not—"

"Don't. Please, just don't say anything."

How could she have been so stupid? Why? She'd all but come into the ear of some poor IT guy, putting in overtime this weekend just to provide her with the information she'd requested! Heaven help her, she was going to have to call him back with some fabricated excuse.

"Come on, Cali, it was just some fun."

"It was my *job*!" she lashed back. "Don't you understand? I'm not like you, Jake. I haven't gotten to where I want to go yet. I haven't reached my goal. I'm still working for it, and stunts like the one we just pulled won't get me there."

He stood back, his brow furrowed in obvious frustration. "That guy isn't going to have a clue what happened here. I disconnected the call before the fireworks started."

"It doesn't matter—this isn't what professionals trying to get to London do!"

Closing his eyes for patience, he muttered a curse.

"Just go. I need—" She needed to burst into tears, and she needed to do it alone.

CHAPTER EIGHT

WITHIN the small sixth-floor office she'd been assigned Cali hung up the phone, disconnecting from the latest status report with Amanda. She leaned back in her chair and spun toward her window, stretching her neck as she observed the late morning activity on the dappled dark waters of the Chicago River below.

Amanda had hinted again about London during their call, causing Cali's pulse to bump at the mention, then transitioned smoothly into her favorite subject. Jake. *Jackson*.

When had Cali last seen him? Really? That long ago? How was he wearing his hair? Wasn't he handsome? Did Cali think he was as funny as Amanda thought he was?

She'd talked to her boss about Jackson as though he didn't exist beyond the context of his relationship with Amanda, but Jake had become the guilty secret that loomed like swollen thunderclouds above her career, ready to burst at any moment. On and on it went, each probe ratcheting the tension between her shoulderblades higher, until finally a bead of sweat had rolled from her temple and dropped into a single small splatter on the top page of her budget report and Cali had abruptly re-directed the conversation to work.

It was too much. Answering politely about a man who made her feel anything but. Feigning indifference over the days that had passed since she'd told him to go. Pretending that guilt and loneliness weren't eating her alive. Jake wasn't to blame for what had happened between them, and, as mad as she'd been, she'd known that all along. The only thing she could blame him for was having the ability to make her weak. Make her want. Make her crazy.

The phone buzzed, jarring Cali back to the present. Leaning over the desk, she connected the line.

"Yes?"

"Pack it in, Cali," came the jubilant voice of Trish, her closest co-worker. "It's Friday, it's noon, and you know I'm not taking no for an answer."

The Chicago office had the afternoon off, and Trish had been planning a department-wide trip to the beach that afternoon.

Cali hesitated, trying to decide if there was any reason she *shouldn't* take advantage of this beautiful day. The sun was shining; the temperature was a perfect seventy-eight. Taking a quick survey of her desk and what awaited her attention, she saw there really wasn't anything she couldn't take home with her for the weekend. Why not? She needed the break, and spending time with Trish might actually keep her from obsessing about a man she shouldn't want.

"I'll be right down."

When Cali arrived in the lobby, she stopped short. Trish, sporting a beach bag, flip-flops, and a tee-shirt that hung off one shoulder, leaned against the front desk, happily chatting up the guard and two guys in suits Cali vaguely recognized from Accounting.

The look was quite a contrast to the soft pink pencil skirt, neatly tailored linen blouse and three-inch heels completing Cali's ensemble.

Trish dismissed the men while surveying Cali's dress. "Have you got your suit on under there?"

She nodded as a flush of heat crept up her neck at the thought of the bikini she'd purchased years ago but never actually worn. This morning, while riffling through her drawer looking for the more conservative tankini she normally wore, she'd realized it had somehow been misplaced in the move. Running late, she'd grabbed the tiny electric blue number with the tags still attached, and a long cover-up to go with it. Unlike Trish, however, Cali hadn't been willing to walk through the lobby in her beach garb and opted to wear work clothes—at least until they got to the cab.

"Perfect. The guys from team six already went ahead to get set up. We'll grab a cab and you can change on the way."

Cali shifted on her feet and glanced back at the elevators, feeling the guilty pull of her project tugging her back.

"Oh, no, you don't." Trish wagged a finger her way. "Amanda said to tell you to stop working for a few hours and to enjoy the sun. So don't make me call her back with the report that you can't follow orders."

"All right, all right," she conceded. "Let's get over there."

By the time the cab pulled to a stop at Oak Street Beach Cali had freed herself from her work clothes in an ungainly display of jutting elbows and pulled hair, and handed them over. At Trish's teasing whistle she'd gratefully donned the cover-up, ready to enjoy an afternoon in the sun.

They walked down the concrete path and onto the wide stretch of flat, light sand beach toward an area spread with blankets, a few coolers, and a beach volleyball net. Cali recognized a number of faces from the office, and waved as one after another stopped to greet her or offer a welcoming smile. Picking a nice spot midway to the water, they spread a blanket, using their shoes to secure the corners in the balmy breeze.

The sun warm on her skin, Cali sat beside the cooler as

Trish dug out sandwiches, bottled water, and a few tubs of cold deli salads. Matt Novack jogged over and edged a seat beside Trish, joking good-naturedly about some mutual acquaintance he'd hoped to get to know better.

Tucking into the meal, they discussed the various "fests", concerts and street fairs abundant throughout the Chicago summer: Taste of Chicago, Venetian Night and Lalapalooza. There were also art fairs, garden walks, air shows, and a veritable plethora of other appealing activities to fill all the free time Cali didn't have.

Still, it was exciting to hear about the masses filling Grant Park, to imagine herself into a life that allowed for such good times. And then, glancing around—at her co-workers, at the gorgeous lakefront with Navy Pier in the distance, the Drake Hotel, and John Hancock building piercing the clear sky above—she realized that somehow this fantasy life was actually hers. For now, anyway.

Cali raised a bottle of water to her lips and took a long draw as a shadow fell over their group, and a pair of legs, tanned, muscular, and lightly dusted with dark masculine hair, stepped up to them.

"Hey, Cali," came the rumbling dark voice from above, setting off a tingly reaction across her skin and through her center. "Was hoping I'd catch you out here."

She froze, knowing instantly who it was. She'd recognize his voice anywhere, and that unique blend of excitement mingling with anxiety only surfaced when one man was in her proximity. Jake.

Her breath sucked in—only she hadn't swallowed the water first, and then she was coughing, sputtering, and losing any shred of cool she might have hoped to retain in front of the last man she'd expected to meet there.

Instantly he was at her side, gently patting her back with

the heel of his palm as he retrieved the water bottle that had spilled all over her lap. "Easy, Cali. You okay?"

Embarrassed, she nodded, looking him over. He was dressed for the beach in a white short-sleeved shirt open to the waist and a pair of long, narrow orange trunks that hugged his muscular thighs as he crouched beside her. "What are you doing here?"

"My afternoon op got cancelled, and Amanda mentioned you were heading down here with a few co-workers. She suggested I crash."

Matt leaned forward to extend a hand, grin wide. "Right on, man. Glad to have you."

Trish chirped in, "Definitely. Have a seat."

They might be glad, but Cali wasn't sure she could say the same. Being confronted with Jake after the way she'd treated him the last time they were together…she didn't even know how she felt. Guilty, embarrassed, anxious, excited—there were too many emotions winding together to form a solid knot in her stomach to identify one over another.

Introductions were exchanged, and then Cali noticed the silence stretching a second too long. She dared a glance at Jake's face.

Mouth tight, brow drawing down, he raked his darkening gaze over her from head to toe and back again. Following his gaze down to her body, she realized the damage one bottle of spilled water could do. Her cover-up was completely saturated, clinging to her like a transparent second skin and advertising Band-Aid sized panels of electric blue, barely covering enough to keep her legal.

Matt gaped from behind Jake, his mouth hanging open, eyes fixed in blatant appreciation. "Damn, Cali. And I didn't get you anything."

How embarrassing. Her arms crossed over her chest as Trish snickered beside her. "Matt, you're an ass."

But it was Jake's reaction that had her heart stalling in her chest. Dark hunger and heat seared over her skin as he stripped off his shirt and wordlessly handed it over to her.

Self-consciously she tugged off the wet cover-up, pulling it free in time to catch his glowering scan of the beach beyond them.

She slipped her arms into one sleeve and then the other, trying not to think about the fact that Jake was now shirtless. About all that bronzed, sculpted torso, the six-pack of hard abdominal muscles or the flex of his bare back. About what the smell of him on the fabric she was wrapping around herself was doing to her body.

She swallowed.

Incredibly, spectacularly shirtless.

Matt chimed in, enjoying the spectacle far too much. "Yep, that shirt's probably a good idea, since you're looking so… chilly."

Cali groaned, blushing bright. "Matt!"

Jake's jaw flexed as he brushed her arms aside and jerked the lapels closed. Grim-faced, he worked the buttons between her breasts, down her belly, to where the last button of the too-large shirt hung between the tops of her thighs. He slowed as his knuckles brushed against the sensitive skin. Forcing her breath to steady, Cali took his hands in hers, pulling them free. If he touched her one more time, with that hot possessive fire blazing in his eyes, it wouldn't matter that they were sitting inches from her co-workers in broad daylight. One more touch and she'd go up in flames.

Their gazes held for an instant before he broke away, jumped to his feet and gruffly announced he was going for a swim. Matt jumped up, laughing, to join him. Nodding toward the water, he clapped Jake's shoulder. "Definitely time to cool off. Let's go, Tyler."

* * *

Some forty minutes later Matt meandered off to hit on some girl wandering along the bike path, and Trish closed her eyes, popping a pair of headphones into her ears. Waves lapped gently against the packed sand, a warm breeze blew in a quiet rush past her ears, and children squealed, racing against the advance and retreat of the cool waters creeping over the beach.

She could get used to this life. Easily.

Jake leaned back beside her, his triceps flexing as he shifted his weight to stretch out his long legs. A smattering of sand clung to the skin around his toes and ankles, drops of water beaded in the dark hair of his legs, while his still-damp suit hugged the muscles of his thighs and the contours of his groin.

She could definitely get used to this life. Much too easily.

She swallowed, forcing her gaze to the distant horizon. There was so much she could make her own here, without risk to her career. It was only a matter of remembering the one line not to cross.

The *Jackson* line. The line where his casual arm around her shoulder reverted to his hands, demanding and skilled, covering every inch of her body.

There were so many reasons not to want him—Amanda, her career, her heart—it should have been easy. And yet she'd begun to question them all. Amanda in particular. Obviously there was an attachment there—one that ran deep. But Cali had begun to question the number of times her boss had facilitated she and Jake meeting. Even today she'd told him where to find her. Ensured Trish would let her know she expected Cali to take the break with everyone else. Or maybe that was just some selfish, destructive part of her, searching for a convenient excuse to justify the reactions she couldn't seem to control.

Jake caught her attention with a jut of his chin toward the cityscape behind them. "How about a coffee and walk?"

Caffeine was always good, and what had happened

between them the week before needed to be addressed. "Sounds good."

Smoothly, he rolled to his feet and stood, offering a hand to pull her up.

When they'd gotten a fair distance from the MetroTrek crowd, Cali brushed at the sand from her hips and took a steadying breath. "I should have called you. What I said— how I acted—it wasn't fair."

Jake cocked his jaw to the side. "I knew how you felt about work and sex. It was a mistake…but only because of the call."

Her heart tripped as she thought about all the reasons she'd been telling herself the entire incident was a mistake. She could have voiced them, but instead let the subject lie.

"So, how's the job going these days?" Jake asked as they headed up to the path.

Cali considered. "Really well, but there are more issues to contend with than we initially anticipated. And I think someone seriously undershot the scheduling projection."

"Yeah? That's got to be frustrating." The skin at the corners of his eyes crinkled as he scanned the lakefront ahead of them. "I'm pretty sure there's a coffee stand right up here. So, will you be able to make it work?"

She glanced at him, shielding her eyes from the sun as an unpleasant thought took root in her mind.

"What?" he asked, that gorgeous mouth pulling up to the side.

Yeah, what? She was paranoid. Only maybe there was another reason Amanda kept throwing them together.

"Nothing…it's just— Well, you're always so interested in my work." It wasn't that he seemed overly curious, only she knew Amanda wasn't above using friends and subordinates to check up on each other.

She couldn't believe that. But still she ran a quick mental tally of every work-related comment she could summon to memory. Nothing that would make her look weak. Nothing unprofessional. Almost nothing. She had to take on faith that the incident in the bar hadn't been recounted.

"Not that I'm complaining," she added hastily, feeling like a jerk for questioning what was probably nothing more than polite conversation. Unless… "And of course I can completely handle the job. It'll require some juggling, but that's what I do."

Jake stopped walking and, catching her hand, turned her to face him.

"Hey." His blue eyes, serious and more intensely beautiful than the bright sky behind him, met hers. "No matter what you say, you know I wouldn't mention it to Amanda, right? She's a friend, but whatever happens or is said between you and me is just that. Between you and me."

The earth seemed to shift beneath her feet as his simple, straightforward words upended her world.

He had to stop touching her, stop searching her eyes as if he knew if he looked into them long enough he'd find the truth she so needed to hide from him. The truth that with their every shared word and accidental touch that same underlying heat from the first night they'd met flared to life.

Only if Amanda *wasn't* using Jake to siphon information about Cali's ability to handle the pressure of the job, then she was back to her initial theory.

This was *Amanda's Jackson.*

Desperately, she took a step back. "Amanda asks me about you all the time, Jake." This wasn't what her boss would want revealed, but Cali had to believe it was better than giving in to the pull of his mouth and arms and his body again.

This disclosure was her last defense.

"She wants to know every time I see you, and she wants to know what we did, what you said, if you enjoyed yourself—

a million little things. Anything she asks, I tell her. There's *nothing* just between you and me. She's my boss, Jake."

The corner of his mouth pulled to the side. And for a moment Cali couldn't tell if he was disgusted, amused or both.

"Then it's time that changed." His thumb swept slowly across her bottom lip, tracing its lower edge in a back and forth rub that left her breath frayed, her mind reeling, and her resolve melting into a molten pool of need. "Where this is going, I don't want Amanda to come."

Desire swirled warm and thick in her belly, and unwanted heat spread across the surface of her skin. She couldn't give in, and yet even as she thought it Jake shook his head, his expression stern. "Don't."

"Don't what?" she managed in a pathetic whisper.

"Don't tell me you don't want this."

Of course she wanted him. But it wasn't as simple as *want* alone.

CHAPTER NINE

THEY'D returned to the beach to find Trish and Matt packing up with the rest of the group. A few minutes later they were settled in the backseat of a cab, riding in strained silence through the downtown city streets. She hadn't answered him, refused to discuss it, and the irritation evident in the hard set of his jaw had her stomach twisting into knots.

A few more minutes and they were wordlessly cutting across the near deserted downstairs lobby to the elevators.

Jake punched the call button and raked his fingers through his hair, his usual smooth, easy motion now jerky with tension. They kept circling one another, trying out different interactions, but it always came back to sex. They couldn't be near each other without having to fight it, and the fighting was getting harder and harder. It had to stop.

"Maybe it's better this way," she mumbled, not realizing she'd spoken out loud until the snap of Jake's gaze—hostile, intense—alerted her.

"What?" he demanded, frustration radiating off him in waves.

She swallowed past nerves and need to meet his stare. "We can't keep on like this. I can't—"

Jake's features hardened, his eyes grew darker, and in their depths she saw a warning that left the words dying on her lips.

But then he dropped her gaze, looked away, and when he turned back whatever threat she'd seen lurking there was gone. It was all easygoing, smooth Jake. Casual, without a care in the world.

Her heart clenched in her chest. It most definitely wasn't a simple matter of want.

Grabbing her hand, he smiled that cocky smile and glanced around, checking out the lobby behind them.

"Hey, come here a second," he said, pulling her gently around the corner to a doored-off alcove that led to the back alley of the building. What could he need to tell her that couldn't wait for the privacy of the elevator car?

The door closed behind them with a quiet thud and then they were alone. Jake stopped, turned to face her, and seized her with a stare that was neither easy nor casual. The beige walls and worn linoleum of the small hallway crowded in around them, as if the space itself couldn't hold out against the man in front of her.

He stood too close, his body too big, his emotions too raw. There in the harsh darkness of his blue-eyed glare she could see everything she wanted to ignore. The urgency, the anger, the heat.

He caught her wrist, closing his fingers around it like a manacle as he pulled her hand to his chest. His eyes locked with hers, daring her to try and hide her reaction to the hot flesh beneath her fingertips.

"What are you doing?" she demanded, her heart racing.

"Making you touch what you can't stop looking at," he growled, pressing her palm flat, drawing her touch over the muscular terrain.

He was so close she couldn't think, could barely breathe. Need twisted low in her belly as she remembered the taste of him, the feel of his hands cradling her. Everything she wasn't supposed to have. Everything she wanted.

This wasn't fair.

Jake searched her eyes and slowly withdrew his hand from hers, bracing one arm and then the other at the wall behind her. He'd boxed her in with his body, but it was her own desire that held her captive.

"It's up to you, Cali. I'm not going to give you the easy out and take the control from your hands." His gaze dropped meaningfully to where her fingers still splayed wide over hard muscle and male flesh.

She swallowed, her mind reaching for justifications and denials just beyond her grasp.

He leaned closer, his words feathering against the shell of her ear. "You know what I see in that look you can't stop giving me?"

Barely a whisper, "What?"

Jake pulled back, bringing them level. "I see you begging me to finish what we've started too many times. But I'm not going to answer to your eyes, sweetheart."

Stifling a moan at the hot pulse of desire beating between her legs, she stared at this man she needed so badly but was too afraid to take.

"You can't make yourself tell me to stop," he growled, leaning forward to burrow his nose into her hair, "but passive acceptance isn't enough." His breath, warm and moist, teased the whorl of her ear as his lips rubbed against the outer ridge. "You're going to have to say it."

A desperate whimper escaped as the tip of his tongue flicked lightly at her lobe and then drew it into his mouth with a hard suction that pulled straight at her core.

"Jake," she gasped, clutching at his shoulders, her hips moving involuntarily against his.

He groaned, circling her waist with his arm and pulling her roughly against him so she pressed against every hard plane and ridge from his thighs to his shoulders. "Tell me," he gritted out between clenched teeth.

Her fingers numbed as they lifted from his chest, rose, and then pushed deep into the dark strands of his hair. There was no doubt, no denial anymore. Only need. Reckless and so intense it resonated through every cell in her body. The need to get closer. The need to feel him—his mouth, his body—against hers.

On a trembling breath, she pulled his face to hers and whispered against his lips, "I want you."

Cali's admission seared over his lips, slammed through his senses, and annihilated all restraint. He kissed her hard. Covering her with his mouth, his hunger, and every possessive claim he would never have acknowledged to exist within him. Their mouths fused and she opened to him. Gave in and gave herself over. No more refusals and skittish retreats.

She was in his arms *now*, beneath his lips, moaning around the thrust of his tongue as her fingers clenched a fistful of his hair.

Man, that felt good.

His hand slid over her bottom, urging her closer. Making her feel him.

"Jake." Her breathless gasp and the tightening of her arms around his neck weren't nearly enough. She'd made him wait, and now that he had her he needed to make her so mindlessly desperate that when his lips parted from hers she wouldn't have senses left to come back to. They'd be obliterated, just like his.

Setting an urgent rhythm of thrust and retreat with his tongue, he nudged a knee between her legs, pushing his thigh against the warm notch there before pulling back. Her breath caught as his hand dipped into her bathing suit, his fingers curving into the slick folds of her sex.

At the touch of his fingertip her knee cocked against his thigh, and Jake pushed inside with one smooth, long stroke.

Cali's broken, desperate cry caressed his lips as her tight wetness encased him so snugly, the sensation of it smoldering through his body straight into his groin.

God help him, she was so tight he was about to lose it just thinking about pushing inside her. Feeling her body ripple around him as he sank inch by inch, until he was buried to the hilt.

Damn it! They were in the hall and he had to stop. Get her into the utility elevator. Upstairs.

Into his bed. Hell, yes.

With incentive like that he should have had them passing the sixth floor already, but then her hand slithered between them. Into his trunks. And the ragged gasp ripping through the otherwise silent hall was his own.

She circled him with her fingers and stroked up his length as she rode first one finger, then spasmed around him as he pressed in a second.

His name, wrapped in another breathy moan, pushed him beyond control—sent him spiraling with only one goal to hold to.

Get inside her.

He had to get inside that slick, wet, begging body. "Feels…good…." she panted as her motions became desperate and her hips tipped further forward, urging him on. "Need you… Please."

Please.

His hand slipped from her bikini, and her heavy-lidded green gaze locked with his, her kiss-swollen lips parting in a silent plea.

Moving between her legs, he grasped the edge of the Lycra panel and pulled it to the side to expose her, to allow him access to the honeyed sweet center of her.

Brushing her hands from him, he caught one leg behind her knee and positioned it to his hip, bringing her into contact with his straining groin. Her hands flew to his shoulders, digging in as he bent his knees, lowered himself to catch the tip of his erection against her in one teasing sweep.

Her fingers clenched. "Jake…."

Poised to breach her body, he held back. "If I don't stop now—" he growled against the sweet soft spot where her jaw met her neck. "I want to come inside you."

"I'm on the pill. Please…I can't wait anymore…I can't stand it."

He pushed in, shuddering at the cry rending the otherwise silent space. Too good. The snug hold of this girl who, before him, hadn't been touched in so long—it was heaven and hell all at once. Gritting his teeth, he pulled back, retreating in measured increments, forcing self-control while she adjusted to his presence within her body. Then another thrust, deeper than before. Harder.

"Good…like that…more…please…please…please…."

Cali's welcoming sighs and straining gasps built warm and wet against the skin of his chest as her body took him deep.

It was pleasure so exquisitely intense it bordered on pain, the breathtaking thrust and agonizing retreat so deliciously destructive her every last defense lay battered, in ruins around her unguarded heart.

"Don't stop…." It was too good. Each kiss of flesh taking her higher and higher, until Jake jerked her standing leg to his other hip, opening her completely to the driving thrust of his body into hers.

Too good. Too much. And she was coming apart in his arms. Her body was seizing around his until she was caught breathless, suspended in pleasure, as his blue eyes bored into hers.

"Beautiful…so beautiful," he gritted out, fingers digging into her thighs, branding her with his need as he drove deep one final time, roaring his release.

CHAPTER TEN

BROWS resting together, their breath came in ragged bursts between them, bathing already overheated skin in a humid caress. Jake's fingers curled around the smooth curve of her hip, his thumb stroking over that sexy bone in front.

What was it about this woman that drained him of his every last sense?

And what about *her*?

Cali was supposed to be the conservative one. The woman with all the concerns and issues. And yet once her switch had flipped—she'd practically been climbing his body to get him inside her.

Damn, it was hot.

But now what he needed was to get her out of this hall. Out of that fantasy, porn-star-next-door bikini and into his bed.

A rivulet of sweat ran from his temple, trickling down his neck. Okay, the shower and then the bed.

Reaching for her hand, he scanned the vacant hallway, once again stunned by his own disregard for privacy and convention. They were making an unhealthy habit of this kind of thing.

Really, he shouldn't be smiling, suddenly aching to crow.

Cali had already adjusted her bikini, and Jake's trunks

FREE BOOKS OFFER

To get you started, we'll send you
2 FREE books and a FREE gift

There's no catch, everything is **FREE**

Accepting your 2 **FREE** books and **FREE** mystery gift places you under no obligation to buy anything.

Be part of the Mills & Boon® Book Club™ and receive your favourite Series books up to 2 months before they are in the shops and delivered straight to your door. Plus, enjoy a wide range of **EXCLUSIVE** benefits!

- Best new women's fiction – delivered right to your door with FREE P&P

- Avoid disappointment – get your books up to 2 months before they are in the shops

- No contract – no obligation to buy

We hope that after receiving your free books you'll want to remain a member. But the choice is yours. So why not give us a go? You'll be glad you did!

Visit **millsandboon.co.uk** to stay up to date with offers and to sign-up for our newsletter

2 **FREE** books and a **FREE** gift

P0EIA

Mrs/Miss/Ms/Mr _____ Initials _____

BLOCK CAPITALS PLEASE

Surname _____

Address _____

_____

Postcode _____

Email _____

The Mills & Boon® Book Club™ – Here's how it works:

Accepting your free books places you under no obligation to buy anything. You may keep the books and gift and return the despatch note marked "cancel". If we do not hear from you, about a month later we'll send you 4 brand new books priced at £3.19* each. That is the complete price – there is no extra charge for post and packaging. You may cancel at any time, otherwise we will send you 4 stories a month which you may purchase or return to us – the choice is yours.

*Terms and prices subject to change without notice.

MILLS & BOON®
Book Club

FREE BOOK OFFER
FREEPOST NAT 10298
RICHMOND
TW9 1BR

NO STAMP
NEEDED!

NO STAMP
NECESSARY
IF POSTED IN
THE U.K. OR N.I.

hung at a respectable level on his hips. "Come on, we'll grab the elevator back here."

She followed silently behind him, her steps dragging their pace until she drew to a stop. "I can't believe that I—that we—" She broke off, searching his gaze as she waved her hand toward the alcove he'd never pass without smiling again.

"I know, another hallway. Sorry—"

Her lips pursed. "No, not that." She glanced uneasily away and the hairs on the back of his neck stood on end. "Hey?" he said softly. "Cali, look at me."

Her hands fell limp to her sides. Shaking her head, she stared up at him, looking suddenly lost. "I can't stop. I tried, but I want you so much. I can't *not* touch you."

Okay, that was good. He would have been positive—except Cali didn't seem very happy about it. His jaw set.

"Jake, I need to explain. I know you don't see it, but what we just did…. God, I didn't even think about what it might mean for you."

What the hell? "Look, this hall's seen enough action today." He grasped her hand and led her toward the back. "We'll talk on our way up."

The utility car was open and waiting. Jake stepped in behind Cali and pushed seventeen. Then, arms crossing over his chest, he forced a neutral tone. "Explain."

Cali's anxious green eyes met his, and after a second she stepped into him. He didn't know what was wrong with her, what her worry was, but with that single step everything fell into place. For once she wasn't pulling away. Relaxing his stance to wrap an arm over her slender shoulders, he held her against him. "Just tell me," he coaxed.

Her body tensed, and she burrowed so far beneath his arm he almost didn't hear her when she squeaked, "Is there any way that Amanda might be in love with you?" *Almost.*

His chin pulled back as he stared down at the amber tumble of curls tickling his skin. She had to be kidding.

He barked out a stunned laugh. "Amanda? You're freaking out about Amanda?"

Cali's fragile green stare turned sharp as the elevator doors opened at their floor. "Yes. The reason I'm 'freaking out' is because I'm afraid my boss—the woman in control of my future and livelihood—is in love with you."

The last thing she needed right now was to have Jake laugh in her face, and Cali was halfway down the hall, clutching her arms across her stomach, trying to still the nerves, before Jake's hand wrapped around her arm. Warming skin chilled by dread, he drew her to a stop.

"Amanda in love with me? You'll come up with just about anything to try and keep us from happening." He was irritated, accusing, as if her concern was some trite whim.

"Don't try to make it sound like nothing, Jake."

"There's no trying here. It *is* nothing. That's the craziest thing I've ever heard. Cali, I thought we'd be past this now, but you're still creating problems, and what I can't figure out is why. Do you get off on the drama?"

Cali took a step back, her eyes locked with Jake's. "No."

That was ridiculous. She loathed drama. Her every painstakingly selected action was taken in pursuit of security and calm. A life she could count on. But how could he know that, when her life had been nonstop chaos since the moment he'd walked into it?

Opening his apartment door, Jake tossed the keys she hadn't even realized he'd retrieved into the dish atop the secretary table, then stalked past her. "So if that's not it—" he turned on her, arms crossed over chest "—then why are you working so hard to keep this thing from happening?"

It wasn't about keeping them from happening. They'd

happened. Hard. It was done and…wonderful. But the fact that she'd stopped fighting Jake didn't mean there wouldn't be consequences. Her stomach sickened. Potentially for both of them.

"What part of 'my boss is in love with you' don't you understand?"

"The part about it not being true," he answered flatly. "Amanda isn't in love with me."

She stared at him, finding her grounding again with a few feet of space between them. "You're a guy. Your kind is notorious for missing this sort of stuff."

"And now she insults my intelligence, too." He stalked across his living room, rested a palm against the wall and glared back at her over his shoulder. "Seriously, what is it about you that I can't just—?" He shook his head and, looking frustrated, left the rest to hang, making her feel like a fool.

"You don't hear what she says, the way she goes on about you," she said, pleading for understanding. "The near threat in her voice when she talks about *her Jackson*. And it isn't just me imagining it. I mean, there's a part of me that's maybe a little unreasonably jealous, but I knew she had it bad for you *before* we even met."

Staring out the window, he asked, "Has she ever said anything even remotely close to 'I'm in love with Jake'?"

"She says she loves you all the time, *Jackson!*"

"Don't start with that," he warned, before blowing a harsh breath out in a disgusted burst. "She loves me like a *sister*. We grew up together."

Oh, please. Enough was enough. Cali stormed across the room and threw up her hands beside him. "Like you grew up with your ex-wife, *her sister*?"

He shook his head, jammed his fingers into his hair and balled them at the base of his skull. "I'm telling you you're wrong. And I swear you know it too. This is just another excuse. Like you not being able to handle a serious relationship. You know that's not what I'm offering. Like you not having *time*. You've got time. I see you *all* the time—as unconventional as the hours may be. Like you not being interested." He waved his hand at her. "I'd say we negated that point downstairs."

Just the mention of it sent a skitter of chills across her skin, tightening her nipples into beaded points. As if lack of interest had ever been the issue. Couldn't he understand her concern?

He moved on her then, his hands going to the two buttons securing the shirt he'd given her to wear. He unfastened them in short order.

"What are you doing?" she snapped nervously.

"Taking my shirt back."

Ignoring his hands, she tried to make him see. "Everything—all my concerns, all my hesitation—has been about my job, but I wasn't thinking about *you*." Her voice was low but steady, even as he pushed the shirt off her shoulders to the floor, cursing under his breath as his gaze raked down the expanse of her very obviously interested body.

"You're making me insane." His eyes, dark like turbulent waters, shot to hers. "Do you have any idea?"

"My career, Jake. I don't date because I put everything I have into doing my job better than anyone else. I fight for every promotion. I nail every deadline. I'm driven to the point that I don't even notice men." She licked her lips, nervous and frustrated. Determined. "Until you. It wasn't a lie or an excuse. It's what I was trying to do. Only when I'm with you…none of the rules apply. Even knowing how Amanda feels about you, I can't resist."

He let out a snort. "Hell, the way Amanda talks about you, I pegged you as having more sense."

"Wha—?"

She squealed as his hands locked over her hips and he tossed her over his shoulder. "Jake! What are you doing?"

His shoulder digging into her belly with each step, one large hand gripping her bare thigh dangerously close to the juncture between her legs, Jake strode down the hall of his apartment, passing several doors before turning into what had to be his bedroom.

Cali arched up, her hands bracing above his butt to see the room he slept in. Slate walls contrasted with tobacco-finished furniture. A charcoal rug stretched across the majority of the floor, and geometric-based lamps sat atop the various surfaces. The room, as she took it in in one dizzying spin from her perched position, was all clean lines and organization. Different from the rest of his living space, but somehow equally fitting.

"We're talking! This—this is crazy."

"I'm done trying to talk sense to you," he answered without slowing. "I'm resorting to alternative means of communication."

Within a few steps they'd entered the master bathroom. Distracted by the fixtures and decadence, she didn't register that the water hadn't been brought to temperature before she was deposited in the shower stall—not until Jake wrenched the dial and an icy deluge rained down from the overhead fixture. Cali danced on her toes, spinning for the door, but Jake caught her shoulders and held her in place as the cool water chilled them both.

"Now, that's better," he belted out, shucking his trunks beside her.

"What are you? Crazy?" she demanded, her lungs tight from the cold. She pushed her hair back, blinking the water from her eyes as she tracked over the hard, bare lines of Jake's naked body. Surely by now she should have been prepared. She'd touched and sampled so much of him, but never all at once. Not like this.

"Aiming for a cooler head," he replied, inordinately pleased with himself. "Thought we both might benefit from one."

She noted his heated gaze and crossed her arms over her breasts, trying to hide the evidence of nipples that had puckered impossibly tighter. But Jake merely grinned, brushing her arms away, and then let his focus drop lower still on her body. "Though maybe we ought to clear this up fast, because I'm not sure how long it's going to last."

He was right. Already the temperature of the water had begun to rise, and with it the heat building steadily within her core.

"Amanda is not in love with me," he said, cutting to the chase.

How could he even know? "But—"

"No, let me just get this out, so we don't have any more misunderstandings or confusion. You need to stop looking for excuses and start using that sharp intellect of yours to put it together. Amanda is not in love with me. She's been setting us up from the start. Trust me on this. I've been through it before. Though I have to give her credit for more subtlety than she usually manages, this is definitely a set-up."

Cali stared up at him, wanting so badly for it to be true. So simple a solution. No one would get hurt. No risk to her career. "Prove it," she challenged, praying he could.

Arching a brow, he gave a thoughtful nod. "Okay. Reason one: she has *never* asked me to do even one thing for any of the employees she's had coming through Chicago before. But you I've got living next door— Time for these to go."

His fingers flicked at her hips and the string ties at the sides of her bikini bottoms were loose and falling open. Her knees snapped shut, but Jake wasn't deterred, his hands already moving to her breasts, thumbs beneath the fabric, pulling the scant cups to the sides so they trapped her bare breasts between them.

He groaned, catching the turgid peaks between his fingers

briefly before moving to untie the strings of her top. As if on cue the three tiny panels of Lycra fell away, leaving her naked beneath the shower spray. Jake followed the streams of water sluicing down her shoulders, breasts and belly with a gaze so intent she could swear she felt his touch. "God, that's nice."

Staring back at him, she couldn't agree more. Every part of her body was wound tight. Her pulse throbbed in time with the ache between her legs. She was already exposed. Already hot. But resolving this was imperative. "You said there was an issue with the temporary housing."

"Fine." Back on task, he pulled the shower gel dispenser from a built-in shelf in the tile and squirted a handful into his palm. "Fair enough. But, for the record, whatever emergency there was, she didn't mention it until *after* I'd told her about the vacancy opening up next door to me."

She liked it, but as proof went it wasn't exactly rock-solid. If she was going to put this behind her once and for all, she wanted something concrete.

Jake pulled her closer and, wrapping his arms around her, began lathering in slow lazy strokes over her shoulders, neck and back. "Reason two: when I told her I hadn't been able to get much time to talk with you this week, she suggested I hit the beach today. Even going so far as to speculate on what kind of suit you might be wearing. She thought white bikini. I went with pink. Just goes to show how fun being wrong can be."

Cali swallowed. That was something. But still….

Jake's hands slipped down her arms to where her hands had come to rest against the muscles of his stomach. She hadn't even realized. She'd gone to rot.

Taking one hand in his, he squeezed a dollop more gel into her palm and pressed it back into his flesh, letting her skim up his chest to that mind-blowing spot that had led to the demise of her control down in the hall. It was even better with soap.

"And Reason three: she's got a picture of me on her desk from when I was a year old. Droopy diaper hanging half off my butt, full-on snaggletooth smile, and saliva covering three-quarters of my face. It's not the kind of love you're talking about."

Cali pulled back, her heart soaring. "Oh, my word! That's *you*?"

Jake closed his eyes, his mouth setting into a hard line. "You've seen it."

Had she ever? This man who ranked Greek god status in front of her had *not* been a beautiful baby. That picture, so prominently displayed in a frame that said "Luv Bug", had been discussed using words and phrases like "unfortunate" and "maybe he'll be smart" by everyone who'd ever crossed the threshold of Amanda's New York office. No one had a clue that the juicy blue-eyed babe in that snap was actually one of the leading cardiac surgeons in Chicago and, as far as Cali was concerned, the all-time sexiest man alive.

Which brought her back to the sexy man himself, staring down at her with those endless blue eyes, a half-smile fixed on his lips. "You realize what I've sacrificed by admitting that picture is me?"

"I do." What she also realized was that, as of that moment, Jake Tyler was hers, free and clear. Tension loosened from around her chest, freeing her for her first unfettered breath in weeks.

Her hands skimmed over the planes of his chest, his washboard stomach, his trim hips and then inward, to stroke the smooth-steel length of him.

His jaw clenched even as he gritted out the words. "So, you believe me about Amanda now?"

"I believe," she murmured, giving in to the seemingly magnetic pull of his body as the water rinsed the last of the suds from their skin. Her mouth opened over his chest, slid across to cover the disk of his tight male nipple. She flicked at it with her tongue, groaning at the sensation of Jake's hands weaving through the wet mass of her hair.

Silky heat pooled within her as the seductive image of making Jake tighten his hold flooded her mind. Hungrily, she kissed down the contours of his torso, licking and sucking a greedy path south.

Jake's gruff warning sounded above her. "Cali…."

But she couldn't stop—wouldn't. "I want…." she whispered, breathing the steam rising off his skin, the clean scent of him. Then she was melting to her knees between his legs, taking what she wanted.

She'd given in, and it felt so good, so free, she wanted Jake's surrender as well.

Licking, tasting, gorging on the erotic fantasy come to life, she moaned around him, her own arousal building exponentially with the masculine sound of restrained pleasure.

"Enough," came his harsh growl as Jake pulled free of her and ducked, swiftly lifting her into his arms. "It's time we did this in a bed."

CHAPTER ELEVEN

CALI was a slick tangle of wiggling, naked perfection as Jake held her soaking wet body against him. Hands devouring the damp terrain of her skin, he couldn't touch enough, couldn't get close enough. His fingers pushed into the hair at the base of her skull, fisting over the wet mass as he pulled her head back, opening her mouth wider to the thrust of his tongue.

He filled her, sweeping through that moist, warm space that tasted like sweet desire. God help him, he had to get inside her again—feel her around him. Hear those breathy sounds she'd make as he took her.

Water streamed from her auburn tendrils, coursing down the creamy expanse of her body, dripping from the taut peaks of her nipples and clinging to the darker curls between her legs.

He carried her to the bedroom, braced a knee at the edge of the mattress and set her down. Her bare chest, glistening wet and tinged with pink where they'd rubbed together, rose and fell in rapid succession as she scooted to the center of the bed, a lust-hazed gleam in her eyes.

She reached for him, but he caught her wrists and pushed her back, following her down. He stretched her hands above her head. Holding her gaze, he adjusted his grasp on her hands, threading their fingers together as he pinned them to the mattress.

"No more running, Cali," he gritted out, sliding against the welcoming hold of her body in a torturous stroke. "No more excuses."

She flexed her fingers, tipping her pelvis to meet him. "I'm not running. And I don't have any excuses left. I don't want any."

"No?" He stroked again. Another tease.

"No. All I want is you."

"Good." Pushing her thighs apart, he opened her legs wider and, wearing his most wicked grin, gave her what she wanted.

An hour later, Jake walked back into the bedroom, a towel wrapped around his hips, chuckling at the sleepy smile on Cali's kiss-swollen lips. "What are you thinking?"

He wouldn't have thought it possible, but a slow blush rose to her cheeks.

He shook his head. "Oh, no. Not for at least another five minutes."

"Five?" she asked, pulling a corner of the sheet up as he neared the bed, making room for him to slip back in.

"Ten at the most. I'm not a machine, Cali."

"Mmm. But if you were, think of the marketing potential."

"Knock it off, lady. You're making me feel cheap." Jake pulled her into his arms, savoring the press of her bare breasts and the spill of tangled curls tickling his chest. Her thigh tucked between his legs.

They fit together.

After a quiet moment, Cali peered up at him. "I know you were right, Jake. I was making excuses. Looking for reasons not to get involved with you." Her fingers dusted over the light hair on his chest, tracing circles on his skin. "I was scared."

He brushed a hand down the length of her back, settling over the flare of her hip. "Was it really so bad last time?"

Cali laughed against his chest, her lips and breath feathering over him, only the sound was anything but light. "Pretty bad. The guy was your average scum. I'm the one who took 'bad' from just plain to monumental."

"I find that pretty hard to believe, sweetheart." He stretched his free arm behind his head, settled into the pillow. "Tell me about it?"

Warm breath rolled across his skin and Cali molded herself closer.

"I dated a man who cheated on me. But before I found out what was happening I made several errors in judgment. I thought I was in love with this guy."

She rested her chin against his ribs and stared up at him with those soulful eyes that made him think of slow jazz and smoky melodies. Eyes he didn't like to think of gazing at another man from a distant past.

"It probably won't surprise you that I wasn't a huge party girl in school. I've always been pretty serious about work coming first, so I didn't have a lot of romantic experience when I met Erik."

Erik. The man who'd had her heart. Her body and trust. Things Jake was suddenly feeling very possessive of. Short-lived as this relationship was destined to be, for now Cali was his. And the idea of another man betraying her was difficult to tolerate.

"He was so excited about everything—really a 'jump into life with both feet' kind of guy. So different from me. I loved it, and I fell for him. Hard enough that I wouldn't let myself see what was right in front of my face. He was cheating and he was using me, neither of which I chose to believe even when the evidence started piling up at my feet. I wouldn't accept that a guy who made me feel so good could possibly be that kind of bad. I turned down an international position to stay in town with him *after* he'd cheated on me. Of course

I believed him that he hadn't, but—oh, man, being proved wrong later—that was tough."

An international position? Like the one she was pursuing now? Was she just catching up to where she'd been?

"Everyone has lapses in judgment, Cali. We always want to believe the best about people we care for. I'm sorry this guy hurt you. He sounds like an ass and an idiot for not appreciating what he had in you."

"Not really. I mean, yes, the guy was definitely scum. But he did appreciate me. He appreciated that I had a skill-set that paid bills more effectively than a mostly-out-of-work actor. He appreciated me enough that when he got a break in L.A. he begged me to give up my job in Boston and go with him. I'd busted my butt all through school to get in with that company, used every reference. People put their necks out for me, swearing I was someone who could be counted on—"

Cali buried her face in her arm, just breathing for a moment. She wasn't done, so he waited, knowing the rest would come.

"I should have told Erik I wouldn't go, or at least held strong and finished the project I'd signed on for. Only this one time when we were arguing about it he asked me what kind of woman put a job before the man she loved, and I…." She dragged in a long breath and turned her head so he couldn't quite see her face. "I thought, a lonely woman." She laughed a little. "In the end, I caved on every front. Not only did I agree, but in order to take advantage of this 'big break' he had I quit with half the notice I should have.

"Apologies only go so far when people are counting on you—I basically burned every bridge I had. So, while Erik was a jerk, I'm the one who really wrecked my life. For some guy who put a ring on my finger and then screwed the girl from the coffee shop in my bed, two weeks after I gave up my career for him."

Jake jolted up. "You *married* him?"

She pulled back, surprised by his reaction. "No. Engaged."

Settling back into the pillow, he tried to release the irrational tension that had snapped into his muscles. Okay, now he got it. This jerk had done a number on her like no other. *This* was the reason she'd been losing her mind about giving in to a relationship that was even remotely tied to her career. "Cali, everyone makes mistakes."

"You just have to learn from them, right?"

He smiled down at her, wondering about the lesson she'd taken from her experience. "Yeah. But you can't keep them from letting you live or you end up going nuts."

"I know. But it's hard for me to let down my guard when it comes to my career."

"Even when you know it's not going to get that serious?" he asked, tensing for her answer.

"I guess it's just felt safer to avoid romantic entanglements altogether."

"Except pretending you don't have the usual human needs doesn't mean they aren't there, building in you like a pressure cooker. Think about the night we met. Your bikini. Hell, the hall downstairs, for that matter. You try so hard to rein in your emotions, needs, anything that could get you into trouble, until suddenly you can't contain it any longer and you find some extreme outlet to vent off the excess." Cali's brow wrinkled delicately and Jake dropped a kiss at the furrow between her eyes. "Or are phone booths your preference for first dates?"

"Jake, that was—"

"I know. An unfair example because of my extreme animal magnetism."

She swatted his arm harmlessly, ending in a slow caress that sent a wave of heat surging through his chest.

"But, magnetism aside, let's assume that's uncharacteristic behavior for you. A little reckless maybe. You've ignored a very real side of yourself, Cali. You are an incredibly sensual, sexy being."

She laughed then, shaking her head in dismissal. "Not quite, Jake."

He stared at her. How could she not know? Not recognize it in herself? Had it just been too many years of denial? Too many times where, when the dam burst, she'd been with the wrong man?

"Cali, don't you feel what it's like between us? That's not just me. Not even close, sweetheart."

"So you're saying that if I tend to this other side of myself—?"

"In moderation, of course. Like I said, I'm only a man."

She rolled her eyes. "Then my subconscious won't sneak up on me, leaving me with a scandalous blue bikini that I'll have to incinerate the next chance I get."

"Bite your tongue. Or better yet" He leaned over and briefly nibbled her bottom lip. "I love that bikini. I'm confiscating it. And you can wear it for me *here* any time you like."

Cali let her head fall to the side, laughing, and then peered up at him again, mischief in her eyes. "Is that so?"

"That's so." His fingers trailed across one slender shoulder, down through the hollow between her breasts to where her heart tripped beneath her skin. "A little romance isn't going to end your career." Then lower still, across her belly, circling once around her navel before continuing the downward exploration. "All I'm saying is let yourself enjoy this while we have it."

Cali arched against him, her eyes drifting closed as a decadent sigh escaped her lips. "Ooh, I am."

CHAPTER TWELVE

THEY burst into Jake's apartment laughing, nearly tripping over each other as he pulled Cali into a quick kiss. Then, stripping the *Sunday Tribune* from her arms, he guided her around to the living room area.

Indulging in a full body-stretch, Cali moaned at the sensation of hard-used muscles pulling long throughout her body. Well-used muscles. Deliciously used. The thought alone had her senses awakening, but already Jake had dropped to the floor—back resting against the front of the leather couch, legs extended before him. A study of casual masculine perfection.

"Front page?" he offered, as she moved in beside him.

She shook her head. "Comics first."

Jake gaped, an expression of disbelief painted across his gorgeous features. "Not World? Or Business? Travel, even?"

Snatching the colorful spread of cartoons from his grasp, Cali rolled her eyes. "I've been having too much fun. Not quite ready to give up frivolity in exchange for the standing of humanity at large."

"Fair enough, sweetheart. But I'm stunned."

Cali laughed him off, but in a way she was as well. Being with Jake made her want to stop and savor the light moments. There would be plenty of time for all the rest later.

Passing the sections back and forth, they read snippets of the articles that interested them out loud. Discussing and then moving on. It was lazy and decadent. Highly entertaining.

Jake's knowledge base was incredible—he knew something about everything, from pop culture to politics to classic literature and everything in between. He was open with his opinions, thoughtful and considering of hers, interested in debating anything and everything. She felt like a starry-eyed schoolgirl, staring at him in awe, marveling at his every inane accomplishment, and wondering if there was anything this superman specimen couldn't do. It was foolish, but she couldn't help but be impressed.

He was incredible.

The whole past week had been.

She'd been hitting the office early every morning to try and get out by seven at night. They'd spent their nights together camped out on his floor or hers, stretched across a couch, laughing and talking, frequently using furniture for purposes it wasn't intended for. Overall, she'd been making up for three years without any life to speak of in the span of one fabulous week.

A dreamy sigh slipped from her lips before she'd had time to check it.

Jake chuckled quietly beside her, folding the Sports section into a neat rectangle and offering it over, while snagging Travel from her lap. "Please tell me that sound had something to do with me."

"I don't know what you're talking about," she said, mentally berating herself for being so completely obvious.

"Really? Hmm…. Kind of a breathy, sexy, desirous sound?"

"Your ego!" At least he hadn't pointed out that said sexy sound had followed on the heels of her staring at him all doe-eyed for the previous five minutes.

"Yeah, well, we've already been over the solution to that one, haven't we?"

Smothering a grin, Cali pushed to her feet and headed into the kitchen. "What was it again? A glass of cold water over your head?"

"Only if you want the next glass down your shirt," he called after her. "Which actually sounds rather interesting now that I think about what you've got on."

She glanced down at the pale pink short-sleeved blouse she was wearing and shook her head. But just as quickly she thought about the white tee-shirt currently stretched across his chest and had ideas of her own.

Get a grip, Cali. She was worse than he was. Way worse.

Pulling out the basket of strawberries they'd picked up at the farmers' market on Armetage and Orchard the day before, she asked, "Want any of these?"

Her refrigerator was stocked with savory herbs, ripe fruit, and vegetables so fresh the earth still clung in places. She loved it.

Jake leaned one shoulder against the wall, his gaze moving hungrily over her as she offered the basket to him. "You know, I have this recurring fantasy about you in my kitchen."

"Really?" she asked, stepping closer to hold one ripe red berry to his lips. His hand snaked around her waist. "Your kitchen as opposed to mine?"

"It involves supplies."

Her body warmed from within. "Like the kind you picked up at the Snappy Store last night?"

His mouth curved into a wicked grin at her mention of his ice cream purchase.

"Maybe you should tell me about this fantasy in more detail."

"Bring the berries and I'll show you instead," he growled, pulling her by the hand toward the front door.

With a pained sigh, Cali shook her head and stopped. "I

can't. I *can't*." She hated to step back from this fantasy, but she had work to do. Work she'd been putting off all weekend. "I want to, but I have to get caught up this afternoon."

Jake bowed his head to her ear, his breath teasing the whorl as he detailed his sensual threat. "What's three more hours, anyway?"

"Not fair," she whimpered, her hands running over his chest as he let out a low, menacing laugh.

"Did someone tell you I played fair?"

Damn him.

Hating to do it, she pushed back. "No. Not today. But, actually, I was thinking maybe I could make you dinner tomorrow. I'm not a half-bad cook, and then after…."

Jake shook his head. "Tomorrow's no good. Meeting with my research partner I can't put off. We've got a conference in a few weeks, and we need to hammer out some details on the talk."

"No problem. Another time."

"Tuesday night?"

As she was about to agree, four sharp trills from Jake's phone cut her off. A quick glance at the message display and his jaw set. "That's the hospital. My patient—scheduled for surgery tomorrow—well, he's going in now."

Jake caught her chin and tilted her face to meet his gaze. The hunger was still there, but she could see his sharp mind engaged in whatever emergency he faced at the hospital. His thumb brushed her cheekbone. "Tuesday night?"

She nodded at his phone, aware of the role their respective jobs would play in making plans. "Let's see how it pans out."

"Nuh-huh, Tuesday," he said, backing out of her apartment, his gaze lingering on her until he let out a frustrated growl and pulled the door closed behind him.

Cali slumped against the refrigerator behind her and slid down to the floor, wondering if the smile she hadn't been able to shake for days would ever go away. This man was beyond perfect. Every time he laced his fingers through hers, every smile, every sexy, depraved, fantastic suggestion, had her aching, bursting with some emotion she didn't want to think about. The way this man made her feel was dangerous. Alive. And ready for more.

Tuesday morning, Cali was suffering the symptoms of withdrawal.

The sleepless nights. The achy body. The near obsessing over the one thing she wanted above all else. Oh, yes. She'd become a Jake Tyler addict, all right, and after less than two days without seeing him she craved a fix that couldn't come soon enough.

She could wait until five. Somehow she felt as if she'd waited her whole life for a man like him. What were eleven more hours?

Unless she went over there right now.

The coffee-maker beeped that it was ready, and she filled her travel mug. At six-oh-five in the morning, she imagined a wake-up call wouldn't garner the reception she'd be hoping for. Better to wait. Besides, her morning was stacked with back-to-back meetings that started in thirty minutes. There wasn't time. Really, there wasn't.

With a deep sigh, she added a splash of milk and a spoonful of sugar, capped the mug, and gave it a swirl as she headed for the door. Work first. Reward—in the form of Jake's naked body colliding with her own—after.

Coffee in hand, Cali locked her apartment and turned for the elevator, dropping her keys into her purse as she walked. The sound of a lock turning ahead had her pulse kicking up. Could they actually run into each other this early? Could she talk him into starting his morning twenty minutes late?

Her body responded to the quiet creak of his opening door like melting butter, with a rich, warm spread of pleasure through her center. A smile slid across her face as her steps quickened, and her head angled as she sought to get a glimpse of the man who made her ache. Was he leaving for work too, sexy in a shirt and tie? Or headed to the gym, sexier still, with a bed-head and clothing he could get sweaty in?

She ran a hand over her hips in a quick check of her clothing. Her makeup was polished, she'd finished it only minutes ago, and she hadn't had more than a sip off coffee so her mouth still held a hint of mint.

Jake's door cracked further and then pulled fully open.

What—?

A woman stood at the threshold. Fumbling with the top-most button of her blouse in a way that revealed the scarlet lace mounding her breasts below.

Blood rushed to Cali's head. Her breath ceased to pull through her lungs and her gut hollowed.

Maybe there was an explanation. Maybe—

The woman was beautiful. Petite, with china-doll-delicate features—blue, blue eyes, and honeyed hair that fell into a soft curl at her breast. She was stylish, in silk French cuffs and low-cut, narrow-hipped charcoal trousers that flared over stilettos. And she was buttoning up her freaking blouse while she stood halfway in the hall. On her way out of Jake's place at barely six in the morning.

Oh, God. Really what kind of explanation could there be?

She was going to be sick.

As Cali managed to put one foot in front of the other and pass the door a new panic set in. This woman's walk of shame was coinciding with Cali's trip to the office. They were going to have to share the elevator to the lobby. Heat crept up her neck, bringing with it a sickening sheen of anxious sweat.

The stairs were at the other end of the hall. It might be worth backtracking. Her breath was coming faster, she realized. No good to hyperventilate in the hall. Someone might call a doctor to assist, and then she'd bludgeon him to death and end up in the clink for the rest of her life.

Get a grip. Get a grip.

Okay. Forget the stairs, forget the elevator, just get out of the hall. She'd hurry back to her own apartment.

From Jake's door behind her, a lilting voice murmured something, and Cali's tension increased tenfold. Jake was awake. If she walked back past his door she'd have to see him.

The only choice was to move forward. The quiet murmur of voices continued.

"…wonderful…felt so good…bed…."

Her chest ached with a flesh-rending kind of pain that ripped through the center of her. While she'd been thrashing in her sheets, frustrated by the idea of having to wait another night to be with him, Jake had been burning up *his* sheets, screwing another woman three walls away. Blood rushed past her ears, and her stomach seized in on itself, threatening imminent revolt.

Her fist knotted against her side as her breath came in ragged, fitful bursts. Damn him. Damn herself for trusting him! Her vision narrowed with her erratic gasps, swamping her in muted sensation. The buzzing hum within her head intensified like a raging swarm of bees until all other sound was drowned out.

Moving toward the elevator, she forced herself forward as an icy calm seeped into her chest, dousing the hot rage and hurt. She'd known better than to get involved, to open her heart again. She didn't have time for feelings. She didn't have time for heartbreak. Chicago was about work, about reaching that next rung on the ladder of success. This was just a painful but blessedly private reminder that she needed to realign her priorities.

Silently, the elevator doors opened. She stepped into the car and turned back to face the hall. The sight of the woman pulling out of an embrace burned into her retinas. The doors slid closed and Cali's reflection stared back at her. Still. Silent. Unblinking.

Her senses returned with the gentle ding as the car stopped at the lobby. With the exception of her hands—her fingers felt as though the tendons had shortened within them and every flex and motion strained—she was coolly numb.

Cali curled her thumb over the lid of her mug and pushed the sip-flap back. Took a swallow of what might have been blistering coffee and sedately crossed the lobby.

She'd known better. But at least this time her stupidity hadn't cost her a career.

Outside, she flagged a cab at the corner and arranged herself into the backseat, work gear piled around her. Punching in the office number, she got her assistant's voice-mail and began dictating a memo regarding the vendor she'd met with the day before.

There was plenty to keep her busy. Nothing that mattered had changed. And so, refusing to acknowledge the emotion weighing heavy in her chest, she swore to herself she was fine.

Tuesday night, Jake hung one hand from the frame above Cali's door and knocked again. She hadn't phoned him back this afternoon, and he was trying to ignore the slight, chalking up his irritation to a day that had been terrible from the get-go. The get-go having shot off shortly after midnight, with the arrival of a woman he hadn't been able to turn away and had spent the better part of the day trying to forget.

Pam. Arriving in a flurry of hugs and kisses and thank-yous for rescuing her—for always being her hero. Tossing around the 'remember whens', giggling on about things they'd done together. Waiting for him to laugh. Waiting for something.

Pam could reminisce all she wanted, and stare at him with those pleading eyes, but the trips down memory lane would never bear the fruit she hoped for. He didn't miss her. Didn't want her back. Couldn't believe after four years of marriage to Paulo she still hadn't quite given up.

Marrying her had been as big a mistake as he'd ever made—a disservice to them both. Which was why, no matter what Pam had done, he knew the blame was shared. He'd been so focused on school and grades and scores and residencies…and Pam had been by his side, pleasant and sweet, since they were sixteen years old. He'd loved her, but it wasn't the kind of love you built a marriage on. Only drifting along, in that comfortable, distracted ignorance, he hadn't realized the mistake until it was too late. Until the unsatisfied expectancy shimmering in Pam's eyes had finally faded and she'd stopped looking to him for something she realized he wasn't going to give her. Wasn't capable of giving her.

And she'd found Paulo.

He hated to be reminded of it. But she was too much a part of his life to ever forget. His youth, his family, his friends, even his career. She'd been there at the start, and there wasn't a person he worked with who didn't know some piece of their history together. Most remembered his wife fondly. Had shared meals and celebrated his triumphs with her. Hell, she was probably having drinks with his partner's wife while she was in town. He'd never actually be rid of her. On some mature level didn't really want to be—had to value her for the bond they'd once shared. But there were other levels not so mature.

If Cali would just open the door he could at least forget about Pam for a while—scrub her from his mind as he lost himself in Cali's warm, sweet body. He needed to cool off. Unwind and let go. No talk. No baggage. No history or mistakes. What he needed tonight was sex and satisfaction—at least until he could shake off the moody disposition weighing him down.

Finally the lock tumbled and the door opened. Only something wasn't right. Cali stood cool and distant, bracing the door in front of her.

"Hey, you okay?" he asked, automatically sidestepping into the apartment and reaching for her.

Cali winced and slapped his hands away, as though the idea of him touching her was beyond repulsive.

What the hell? Jake took a step back, scanning the apartment around them for some clue as to what this was about.

"I saw her." Her mouth pinched shut. The lips he'd envisioned as a balm for the day he hadn't believed could get any worse flattened into an unforgiving line.

Saw who? But then it clicked. He ought to know that disappointed glare anywhere. It spelled only one thing. *Betrayal.*

Of course—she'd seen *Pam* leaving his apartment.

He shook his head, weary from too many hours of bull. He didn't need this. "Take it easy, Cali. It's not what you think."

Coughing out a laugh, she threw her head back in disgust. "Right. And where might I have heard that before? Sorry, Jake. What's that saying? 'Been there, done that, bought the tee-shirt'. So save it."

His jaw clenched, teeth gritting in a series of slow pops as the resentment that had been simmering just below the surface all day threatened to erupt. "Listen. The woman you saw was Pam—"

"*Pam*? Perfect," she cut in. "Wow, let me tell you that makes it even better."

He knew where her frustration was coming from, logically, but she wasn't giving him a chance to explain and he'd had enough.

"I can't believe I thought you were different—"

And then he saw it. Pain too deep. Feelings too real. His eyes snapped shut, wanting to block out the sight of her emotions, but he'd already seen them. Knew what was there. A seed of resentment took root in his consciousness. She had no right berating him like this. None. She wasn't his wife. She was barely his girlfriend!

"I thought that we had something! That there was a chance—"

"That's enough, Cali." His voice was harsher than he'd intended it, but the result was immediate silence.

"You assume too much about the claim you have on me," he stated flatly, daring her to object.

Her head jerked back as though he'd slapped her. But he wasn't done. "Have we ever discussed exclusivity? Even once?"

"That's garbage," she accused, her voice hoarse with betrayed emotion. "We were sleeping together. You acted as though—as if—"

"I acted as if I cared about you. And I do."

"Funny way of showing it."

"Actually, I think I've been pretty good at showing it. Specifically in coming over here—regardless of the fact that you didn't return my call today—because we had plans for dinner. Even though I'm beat to hell after spending the better part of the night dealing with my ex-wife's hotel crisis and acting like it didn't bother me to have her crashing in my guestroom when, honestly, seeing Pam at all frustrates the hell out of me."

Cali blinked back at him, her lips parted in silent understanding. After a beat, she shook her head. "I thought—"

"Yeah, I know what you thought. But don't lump me in with the bad choices you've brought home in the past. I don't screw around on the women I'm sleeping with, no matter how casually. Not while we're together. It's not my style. Never has been."

"Jake, she was buttoning her blouse— I— What was I supposed to think?"

"I don't know, Cali, have you even *met* me?" He was raking her over the coals about Pam, but that wasn't what this was about. She shouldn't have looked at him like that. Why had she let him see it? But suddenly all the things he'd been refusing to acknowledge because being with Cali felt so damn good were too hard to ignore. She'd stopped running from him to protect her career. It was what he'd wanted, but he hadn't realized the risk she'd thought she was taking when she gave in. If she'd been right about Amanda—

She swallowed, let her gaze run the length of the room before daring to meet the challenge of his. "I'm sorry."

Stepping forward, Cali searched his eyes, her own filling with liquid relief as she reached for him. Catching her hand an inch from his cheek, he stopped her, leveled her with a steady stare.

"Look, it's been a hell of a day. One that I can't wait to be done with."

"Don't you think we should talk about this? What you said? I know you were upset—"

He waved her off, hating that aching look in her eyes. "I'm going to call it a night, get out of here and get some rest."

She blinked up at him, and then, as if suddenly understanding, took a step back, her cheeks running to pink. "Okay, I'm— Sure. Okay, then."

"Tomorrow." He leaned in and brushed her cheek with a perfunctory kiss. "I'll see you tomorrow."

CHAPTER THIRTEEN

IT WAS nine-thirty the next evening before the knock came at her door. Cali had been useless all afternoon at work, and after checking her watch every minute and a half for an hour, she'd finally bolted for the door at five. She needed to feel his arms around her. Needed to hear his laugh. And all his sensible, calming, smooth talk reassuring her that everything would be okay. Only Jake wasn't home, and as the hours had passed, she'd begun to panic. Now her nerves were shot, and as she jolted from her perch on the couch she dumped her files to the floor.

With a quick sweep, she haphazardly collected the mess and then raced to answer.

"Jake," she sighed, when she finally set eyes on him.

Running a hand over his jaw, he cocked a smile at her. "Sorry it's so late. Got hung up in a surgery."

Saving lives. If a man had to keep her waiting for hours, having an excuse like that certainly took the sting out of it. "I'm just glad you came. I was worried—after last night—"

"Hey, don't," he soothed, drawing her under his arm. "I said I'd come."

A pinch of warning prickled at the back of her neck, but then slipped away with the soothing stroke of Jake's hand over her hair.

"Can I get you a glass of wine or a beer?" she offered, dodging the confrontation under the guise of good manners.

"No, but don't let me stop you."

She didn't need a drink. Just a resolution of this whole messy business.

If only she knew what to say next—or if only Jake would say something. Ease the tension and put them back on track. But he didn't say anything. Didn't joke or laugh. He merely stepped away from her to shrug out of his suit jacket.

Knowing there wouldn't be any smooth introduction to a subject as uncomfortable as the one she had to broach, she dove in. "Jake, I'm so sorry about yesterday."

There. She'd begun, and it wasn't nearly so bad as she'd expected. Now Jake would volley back, and in no time they'd have everything behind them. Her stomach would stop twisting into anxious knots, she'd be able to choke down more than a single bite of food at a time, and they'd pick up where they'd left off too many days ago with an embrace that lasted the whole night through.

Jake tossed his jacket over the arm of the couch, tugged at his tie with a series of practiced jerks that left it hanging free at his neck, then propped a shoulder against the wall. The portrait of casual comfort and relaxation. Only the edge of alertness in his eyes as he tracked her progress across the room—as if he were trying to gauge her fragility—told her it wasn't so.

"We both said some things—we need to talk about them."

The way he was watching her had her heart sinking slowly in her chest. "I know. We do." She'd thought about little else all day. Trying to make sense of how something going so right could suddenly go so wrong. She crossed to the couch, trying to adjust herself so she wouldn't appear as tense as she was. But when Jake dropped into the cushions beside her and began rubbing her shoulders with one hand it was fairly obvious she'd missed her target. And then, worse yet, he abruptly stopped, as if he hadn't meant to touch her at all.

And just like that every one of her senses went on alert. The haze of frustrated confusion that had plagued her throughout the day vanished as she realized with sickening clarity what was about to happen.

Breakup.

No. That didn't make sense. He couldn't be ending it. What they had felt so right, like nothing she'd ever known before. It was new, yes, but for the first time in her life she felt as if all the pieces had found their proper places. What had happened because of the Pam thing was a…a blip. Certainly she'd misjudged him, and he was disappointed, let down that she hadn't had more faith. That she'd lashed out before giving him a chance to explain the situation. But he had to consider the circumstances.

She couldn't be the only one feeling that what they'd started was worth a bump in the road.

Forearms resting on his widespread knees, Jake let out a slow breath and dropped his gaze to the floor. "Look, Cali, I'm not going to marry you."

"What?" She let out a stunned laugh. Maybe this was going to be easier to resolve than she'd thought. Marry her? That was ridiculous. Marriage hadn't even crossed her mind. "I—I didn't— I wasn't—"

"Really?" He spoke softly, but there was an unyielding edge to his words. "Then what was it you thought there was 'a chance' for last night?"

Oh, well…that. Her arms crossed defensively over her chest. "I don't know. We have a connection. Something… special. I wasn't plotting a wedding."

His expression said, *Not yet,* and before Cali could protest he went on to drive the point home. "Okay, not a ring and ceremony then, but the lasting kind of emotion that goes with it… I saw it in your face, in your eyes. I could see it tonight when you opened the door. You looked at me like you wanted forever. The way you're searching my eyes right now— Cali, you're looking for something in me that isn't there."

"That's not true." She leaned forward, took his hand. "Jake, I'm not looking for anything I didn't see there before. I'm not talking about marriage. I don't know about forever, but there's something real between us. That's all I want."

"It's not love. I told you from the start it couldn't be. Never will be."

Cali's throat tightened as she met those clear blue, beautiful, unwavering eyes. What had happened between them was still so new, so completely wonderful. It was this incredible surprise she hadn't had time to put a name to, let alone consciously examine it to determine how deeply her feelings ran. And yet with that simple, straightforward declaration she felt the brutal loss of it to the very bottom of her soul.

Her breath sucked in on a hiss. She'd been a fool. And the pained expression on Jake's face said that he was seeing her recognition.

The worst kind of fool.

He'd told her—warned her—from the very first night, but somewhere along the way she'd forgotten. Let her heart take the lead in a relationship that was supposed to remain skin-deep. And now Jake was looking at her as if this was goodbye. Not because she'd accused him of sleeping with another woman and once again jumped to the wrong conclusions, but because he'd seen in that moment when she'd been proved wrong the purity and depth of her relief. He'd figured out something she hadn't even admitted to herself.

"Cali, you're too invested in this."

"No." The harsh denial had left her lips before her brain

had time to process the decision she'd already made. The answering silence spoke as loudly as the doubt written across Jake's face. But she wouldn't let him go. Not after having only the barest taste of being with him. Just enough to let her know how desperately she needed more.

She didn't need him to love her. She'd lived without it for so long, and she could live without it from Jake. Because whatever it was he'd been giving her this last week, and even before that, was enough. Was wonderful. All she needed was just more of that. Being with him. Laughing with him.

"It doesn't have to be love."

Clearing his throat, Jake leveled her with a heartfelt stare. "This was supposed to be a fling. *Just* a fling. Something it seemed like we both needed. Wanted. A feel-good, sexy good time between two consenting adults who were clear from the start they weren't looking for something serious."

She could see the banked heat behind his stare. The desire was there, burning in him the way it always burned in her. Only he was fighting it. Being careful of her.

"I don't want to hurt you."

"And I don't want this to end." She wouldn't let it.

The wheels began to spin as problems and solutions sped through her mind. Costs and returns. Needs versus wants. Every kind of workaround. Cali had made her career of thinking past problems to meet her goal. This time she'd do it for herself—and just that fast she had a plan.

Her seeing Pam, coupled with his realizing how deeply Cali cared for him, had pushed every commitment-phobic button he had. She just needed to put them back on safer ground. Give him the space to get comfortable again and everything would be fine. She could do that.

"You're right. Maybe I got carried away." She let out a cool laugh she only hoped sounded more convincing than it felt. "I mean, let's face it, you're a lot of fun."

Jake's shoulders stiffened, his brow drawing down as he studied her. He'd caught the change, but didn't trust it.

Balanced at the edge of the couch, she forced her posture to loosen. Slid one leg over the other, positioning her knees at a sharper angle toward Jake as she leaned back on one hip into an exaggerated seductive pose that caused the hem of her skirt to inch up her thigh and Jake's intent gaze to follow.

"I get that this isn't about forever. Okay. I don't need forever. I need London. But before I get there…" she reached down to flick a little piece of nothing from the turn of her ankle, allowing her fingers to run a short distance up her calf "…I wouldn't mind having a little more of you."

"Cali." He shook his head, closing his eyes with a rough groan. "I don't believe you. You're talking like a different woman than the one who was sitting here with me, her heart in her eyes, two minutes ago."

"I'm talking like a woman who can understand the concept of having a good time." Cali leaned further into Jake's space, noting the whitening of his knuckles as her breath feathered over his ear. "We have fun, Jake." Her breasts brushed against his arm. "I won't let you hurt me."

"Cali," he groaned, an instant before dragging her across his lap to straddle his thighs. Crushing her mouth with his kiss, demanding more. She opened to him, took the thrust of his tongue with a desperate moan, shivering as he licked once and again. Everything would be fine. Jake was holding her. So strong. So right. Gripping her with hands that sought to touch every part of her at once. Devouring her with the kisses of a starving man. How could he have thought they could end this?

He pulled back with a harsh curse, his fists balling in the

bunched fabric of her skirt. A question stood clear against the stark heat of his gaze.

She nodded once.

"It's a fling, Jake." All confidence. No emotion. "So make me feel good."

Jake wrenched the tap closed and stood naked in his shower, chest heaving, muscles bunched, glaring at the wall.

His palm hit the tile with a resounding smack. How the hell had he ended up in her bed, in her *body*, spilling himself inside her, when he'd stepped through her door with every intention of making a clean break and walking straight out.

But that was not how it had gone. He'd started to tell her goodbye, and she'd looked at him with those gorgeous green eyes and told him she wanted him. Didn't need more than he had to give.

There was no way she was as cool as she was playing it. And he'd known it even as he'd watched the words fall from her lips. But that had been part of the problem. He'd been watching her lips. That mouth. Thinking about how it felt moving over him. And when she'd crossed her legs….

She'd done it on purpose, knowing he couldn't be within fifty feet of her without wanting to pin her against the nearest flat surface. And then that unbelievable concession. She'd suggested a fling, and he'd snatched it from her fingertips so fast he hadn't even realized what he'd done until Cali was spread over his lap, moaning into his mouth. And two hours later he'd staggered out of her bed, already half hard for her again, dishing up some lame excuse about not spending the night to avoid any confusion.

Nice guy. He could kick his own ass for letting things get so far out of hand so fast.

He dried off and whipped the towel at the hamper in

disgust. He was always so careful. Picking women with an innate understanding that their relationship wouldn't extend beyond passing a few evenings together—sharing some spectacular food at chic restaurants, a little intelligent conversation, followed by a few rounds of no-strings sex. Not women who'd taken a three-year hiatus from dating and all but screamed from their every action that they wouldn't be able to keep the line between physical and emotional intimacy from blurring. From confusing lust with something— something more.

He'd been off his game with Cali from the start, intrigued by the novelty and challenge of so many conflicting signals coming from such an enticing package. Stop and go. Yes and no. Sexy and shy. The good girl who did bad things. There was only one signal that remained steady, burning bright. That single beacon he hadn't been able to lose sight of. The smoldering heat between them was a constant. Whether she was enraged or listening attentively, telling him goodbye or laughing in his arms, it never cooled—and that should have been warning enough.

But he'd liked it. Too much.

And, ego-driven jackass that he was, he hadn't recognized the danger of breaking his own rules. He'd gotten caught up in the chase, working for her in a way he couldn't ever remember working for a woman before. Her hesitance to get involved had been exciting, challenging, and had given him a false sense of security about her unwillingness to commit.

Stupid.

Because of course he'd caught her. And, blindly reveling in the thrill of conquest, he hadn't even noticed when she'd begun bombarding him with one incredible sensation after another. The sight of those green eyes glinting with mirth. The sound of her laughter whispering through the night. The feel of her sigh washing over his chest as she drifted off to sleep. The scent of her hair as he woke with his nose buried in the soft tumble of it. The taste of abandon when she gave in to his kiss. She was a full-scale assault on his senses, and he'd been heedlessly following this feel-good tug at his heart until he was teetering at the edge of that sinkhole of contentment he'd spent the last four years so deftly trying to avoid. Poised to wade in.

And then to discover she was already there!

What a mess.

Dressing for a day of patient appointments he hadn't had enough sleep to look forward to, Jake jammed his legs into a pair of khaki trousers, and buttoned up a white Oxford shirt. As mad as he was at Pam for dropping out of thin air with her usual sense of selfishness and bad timing, it was more than obvious he owed her one this time. It hadn't taken more than a few hours with his ex-wife within cursing distance to clear his head of the emotional fog that had settled there. To realize how complacent he'd allowed himself to become and to figure out that he needed to stop what was happening with Cali before it spun any further out of control than it already had.

Okay, so he hadn't managed to end the relationship. She'd made it too easy, given him too many ways to justify keeping what he wasn't ready to give up. Yet. But this thing between them—no matter how they redefined the boundaries—wasn't going to last. He didn't want it to. And Cali was going to London—or wherever they assigned her next. She wasn't staying in Chicago. Hadn't even made any noise about wanting to stay. At least that was something.

Yeah. Right.

Draining his single-serve espresso in one scalding gulp, he thought of the three-day conference coming up in Colorado.

Three days. More like five if he worked the travel and packing right. It could be a natural breaking point.

They'd have a couple of weeks before he left. Time to get each other out of their systems—though he sure had a way to go before he got her out of his—time to have some fun. To make up for a few of those years Cali had gone without.

The truth was, he wasn't that phenomenal a catch for a woman with any kind of emotional capacity. Within a few weeks Cali would figure that out for herself. She'd be happy when he took off, and relieved when they didn't pick things up after he got back.

It was win-win. For both of them.

Right.

He stalked out into the hall, still carrying too much tension from the night before. Juggling his keys in his palm, he ended up somehow twisting the apartment key so its teeth caught in the smaller ring of his car key and wedged in place.

Come *on*. There—he almost had it. How in the hell—? "Damn it!"

"Good morning to you too."

Jake jerked his head around, to find Cali peering over his shoulder, amusement glinting in her all too alert eyes. She was wearing a creamy silk blouse and a knee-length skirt that might have made another woman look like the school principal, but on her….

"Cali, hey—"

"I hate it when that happens. Here, let me try." Casting him an impish wink, she reached around him and plucked the keys from his hand. "I have less emotion invested."

Jake barked out a laugh, catching her lighter mood *and* the straightened keys as she tossed them back. "My hero," he said, locking the door and then turning to wrap an arm around her shoulders—stopping himself an instant before he stiffened, gave himself away, made them both uncomfortable.

That wasn't going to happen. Just like pulling her into an embrace and backing her into his apartment to spend an hour or so in bed wasn't. Shake it off.

"Why don't you let me buy dinner tonight as thanks?" He'd take her out to someplace cool. Give her a few Chicago experiences to remember him by. He glanced down at the vee where the silk of her blouse overlapped, shifting with her each step down the hall. Give her a few more when they got back.

"Dinner sounds terrific. Is seven-thirty okay?" Cali peered up at Jake as they walked down the hall together, acting as if last night their relationship hadn't been hanging in the balance. As if they hadn't made love, only to have Jake rise minutes later to return to his apartment rather than sleep with her, as he had before. She'd seen him waiting for her to freak when he'd told her he thought it might be "a good idea".

It hadn't seemed like a good idea at all, but she'd simply smiled and stretched, offering a teasing glimpse of her body as the sheet slipped below one breast. And then she'd wished him sweet dreams, acting as though she hadn't seen his gaze riveted to that swell of exposed skin. It had been a head-game. Something she'd have sworn she didn't have the first inclination to play, but she needed him to know she was fine…*and* she wanted him to hate to leave.

Jake flashed his even white teeth in approval, though somehow it didn't seem quite like the easy smile he always seemed so ready to give. The blue pools of his eyes didn't reveal anything of his thoughts or emotions, just reflected light back at her in a way she found more disconcerting than when he'd gotten up to leave the night before.

She could handle this.

"It's a date, then," he said, jabbing at the call button for the elevator.

Fighting the tremble trying to work its way through her lips, she nodded, quickly looking away. *It was a fling*.

CHAPTER FOURTEEN

A WEEK had passed, and Jake had taken Cali out nearly every night. This evening they were seated in the tightly woven rattan chairs of Le Colonial, where the presentation of French-Vietnamese cuisine was as memorable as the unique blend of flavors—fresh and hot, sweet and tangy—that burst over the tongue. They'd sipped lemongrass martinis, surrounded by banana trees and potted palms, with Jake feeding her bites of wok-seared monkfish with chili, lemongrass and peanuts as he charmed her with childhood stories of Amanda, making her laugh until her stomach hurt.

He was the personification of the perfect date. His attention never wandered. His conversation never waned. Flawlessly, he entertained and enthralled from start to finish—and yet something fundamental was lacking in their interaction. Something she'd all too briefly enjoyed before helplessly watching it slip from her fingers.

Of course this was what they'd agreed to—only a part of her had hoped this methodical, smooth-talking charmer would revert naturally back to the man she'd fallen for. She'd believed he simply wouldn't be able to deny the connection. But she'd been wrong. Jake was as adept at maintaining the emotional distance between them as he was at closing the physical.

Cali hadn't caught on to the subtlety of his manipulation at first. All the extravagant dates—the opera, the Steppenwolf Theater Company, dining out at Chicago's trendiest and most renowned establishments. He chose carefully, ensuring that, whatever the setting, something about it—an invitation to join co-workers, raucous noise, required silence—insulated them from the kind of conversational depth that had so naturally developed between them before. No more dinners on the floor, where the food cooled ages before they stopped talking long enough to remember to eat it. Of course they still talked, but the chit-chat came from a place as open to a passing stranger as it was to her.

One element of their interaction, however, had not diminished. The heat. No matter what their activity, with each passing moment the tension between them built. A glance. A touch. A knowing smile. Each heightened the awareness. The arousal. The anticipation. Until desperation overwhelmed them, and the date ended with Jake backing Cali into her apartment, with her clawing at his clothes, climbing his body—

But, regardless of the intensity of it—their desperation to have it—it was just sex. Incredible sex. Addictive sex. The kind you wouldn't dream of turning your back on, regardless of the hollowing ache that lingered for hours once it was over. Once Jake had pulled on his clothes, dropped a kiss at her lips, and gone home to sleep alone.

A fling. This was how it worked.

Cali dabbed her napkin at the corner of her mouth, studying the Southeast Asian décor surrounding them. "You never should have brought me here. It's almost too cruel to give me a taste of something so incredible, knowing I'm going to have to give it up so quickly!"

Her eyes danced around the interior, hopping from the delicate fans suspended high above, to the louvered shutters lining the room, then the scattered photos of 1920s Saigon, before landing back at the tight expression on Jake's face. His guard was up, impenetrable eyes showing her nothing but a defense erected against her. Immediately she recognized the problem, the way he might have taken her casual comment.

She smiled blithely. "I'll be dreaming about this place for the next six years."

See? No big thing. No deeper meaning intended. No need to shut her out so completely.

Or, at this point, did it really even matter?

But then Jake's thumb grazed over her wrist in a slow circle, and every cell in her body responded to the touch, pulsing with a need to get closer. Her eyes met his—still impenetrable, but smoldering with sensual promise—so different than mere seconds ago.

Yes, it still mattered.

"If we get out of here—" his fingers dropped beneath the edge of the table, stroked once along the back of her knee "—I'll give you something to dream about for the *next ten*."

Trish waved a slow hand in front her face, beckoning with an amused smirk. "Earth to Cali…come in, Cali?"

She snapped to attention, heat immediately rushing to her cheeks with the guilty knowledge of where her mind had drifted. "I'm so sorry, Trish. Where were we?"

"Confirming that we've got RSVPs from all the criticals for tomorrow's meeting," Trish answered patiently.

Right. The meeting. "We do—thank you."

What was wrong with her? Not only was she wasting her own time, but now she'd wasted Trish's as well. It was inexcusable, and so completely out of character Cali felt herself brimming with frustration.

"Great, we're all set." Trish piled up her folders, notepad

and PDA, then shifted her weight to one hip, relaxing into the stance. "So, how's it going with your hot doc?"

Cali swallowed, busying herself with stacking a bunch of jumbled papers she was going to have to sort out as soon as Trish walked out the door, simply to avoid the eye contact. "Good. Very good."

"That's nice."

"Mmm-hmm."

Trish waited her out, until Cali relented and met her questioning stare. "Okay, what?"

"You seem a little tense this week, is all."

Cali immediately ducked, pretending to search for something under her chair to try to give herself a moment. Oh, hell. She was losing it. Slipping at work, when so much hung in the balance. Who else had noticed? Had word gotten back to Amanda?

"I see you flipping out—just chill. It's not like you're wearing a billboard or something, but I work more closely with you than anyone else." Trish grinned as Cali dared a glance her way. "And I'm very sensitive to romantic strife."

Straightening in her seat, Cali pulled it together. "We're not serious enough to have romantic strife. I'm totally fine."

Trish eyed her with a delicately arched brow. "Really?"

Cali swallowed, sat back in her chair, knowing full well the plastic smile she'd forced to her lips wouldn't do a thing to hide the melancholy she felt inside. "Really."

"Okay, I can see you don't want to talk about it. But you know I'm around, whenever, if you need me."

She nodded. "Thanks, I appreciate it."

"Just don't forget it." Trish turned on her heel and left.

The office door swung shut and the stiff smile fell from her lips. She'd been tense. Distracted. To the point that a co-worker had identified it. This was exactly what she'd been trying to avoid for the past few years. Letting a relationship interfere with her career. So Trish hadn't been criticizing her work as much as noting a change in her temperament? Still it was just a matter of time before it got in the way. And she and Jake weren't even fighting.

There wasn't enough emotion involved to fight, she thought with a stab of heartache.

Her mind drifted back to Jake, so quickly picking up where she'd left off before Trish had reminded her she was still in a meeting.

He'd taken her against the wall immediately inside her apartment. Her silk blouse hanging from her wrists like a sensual bind, lace panties pushed to the floor, skirt bunched at her waist. They hadn't gotten any further than that. Hadn't been able to. It had been erotic. Explosive and intense. But even as he'd taken her to new heights of pleasure she'd felt the void between them growing. A distance that hadn't been there even the first night in the bar.

Against the wall.

So much the same.

Entirely different.

He'd shut her out. Kept his mind intent on the choreography of seduction, enslaving her with his touch while his heart remained disengaged. He wasn't the same man who'd looked at her with his soul in his eyes, given her a taste of something she'd never dreamt to have. And, after years of being numb to the needs of her heart, suddenly the organ she'd previously refused to acknowledge felt hollow and deprived.

Her sense of loss didn't make sense.

She'd told Jake she could live with it. She should be relieved. The fact that Trish had been aware of her tension at all should be reason alone to embrace an emotional retreat.

So why did she feel she couldn't?

* * *

It was after twelve, and moonlight streamed in through the window, casting Cali's rumpled form in blue and silver hues. A sheen of sweat coated his skin, his heart slammed against his ribs, and the blood was rushing so fast past his ears the sound was nearly deafening.

After tonight's sexual Olympics he'd had to carry Cali back to her bed, and it had taken everything he had to force himself to crawl back out of it. It wasn't any half hopeful look fading from her eyes that made his exit difficult—that had stopped days ago. It was out-and-out muscle fatigue.

The sex had been *insane*.

Cali let him take her beyond all boundaries, giving her body completely. It had been hot. And yet, no matter how far he pushed her, how long he held back, how explosive the release when he finally gave in to it, satisfaction remained elusive.

Something was off.

He was irritated. Dissatisfied. Uncomfortable in his own skin. He wanted to believe it was the waning of the relationship, that he'd tired of the time he spent with Cali. Except it wasn't true. He couldn't seem to stay away from the one woman he was trying to let go—even now when she'd begun to make it easier for him. Adding distance of her own. Shielding her emotions more effectively.

But still, every night....

The conference was coming up in a few days. He'd end it then. No more excuses or extensions. And when he got back, life would be back to normal. He'd have gotten her out of his head and from under his skin.

He'd be able to breathe again without feeling the ties of commitment binding his chest.

Cali let out a quiet moan, her hand sweeping blindly over the empty sheets beside her.

Looking for him.

His jaw clenched as a tiny frown marred her lovely face. He should go.

Only looking down at her, curled slightly into herself, the moonlit contours of her body visible beneath the sheet, he just wanted to feel her against him again. His jaw set. He just wanted *her* again.

He climbed back into bed. Not to spend the night.

Jake aligned himself front to back with her. Warm breath and a soft sigh feathered over his arm where he'd wrapped it around her, tucking her into the contours of his hardening body.

"Once more," he whispered into the mass of curls at the nape of her neck. "I need you again."

"Mmmm." Her back arched, her bottom pressing into him as she reached one sleep heavy hand over her shoulder to sift into his hair.

His eyes closed as he drew in her scent. Feminine sweetness. Cali.

Sliding into her from behind, he buried himself in that soft, sweet place.

Yes.

This was where he wanted to be.

Maybe if he went slow enough, lingered, he'd lose himself—find that elusive bit of peace that seemed to always be there, hovering at the fringe of his consciousness, but still just out of reach. He was as close to it as he'd been in weeks, so deep inside her. Listening to her quiet mewls, feeling the beat of her heart beneath the palm of his hand. He could almost reach it. So close…. So close….

"Jake," she whispered, just this side of half asleep.

Just until the conference.

CHAPTER FIFTEEN

"ARE you packed?" Cali called from the kitchen, uncorking a bottle of Pinot Grigio at the counter. Her hands trembled as she poured two glasses.

Jake stood by the bank of windows, looking out over the lakefront below. There was a brooding quality to him she couldn't miss and her belly tensed, bracing for something she'd sensed coming for days—something she didn't want to face but knew couldn't be ignored any longer. This was it. The end.

"Pretty much. A few suits, shirts and ties."

Crossing the room, she handed him a glass of wine and took a steadying sip of her own. The vintage, a crisp, light selection, one of her favorites, tasted bitter on her tongue. "So, when are you going to be back?"

"Thursday," he answered, without elaboration.

No talk of calls or plans, because there wouldn't be any. Just a weighty silence, full of meaning.

"Cali, I care about you."

She nodded, her fist tightening around the stem of her glass.

With a bracing breath, he met her eyes. Soulful, intense, unwavering. "But being with you it's just too easy to fall into the kind of pattern I want to avoid. I don't want a commitment. I don't want the heavy emotion. I don't want the *need*—"

"I get it, Jake. I do. I care about you too." More than she wanted to. More than she ever should have. Her chest tightened, her eyes stinging with tears she wouldn't shed. Why did this hurt? She'd lost the man who'd swept her away weeks ago. And yet a part of her had continued to hope. But she knew better now. She understood. This was for the best. For both of them. "It was a fling. It was fun." Her chest constricted as she forced the stubborn words past her lips. "But it wasn't going to last forever."

"Good talk, Jake." A colleague clapped him heartily on the shoulder as another stopped to shake hands on his way out of the conference hall.

Jake returned greetings, discussed techniques and practices, caught up with old friends, but all the while Cali remained, ever-present, in the back of his mind.

He couldn't stop thinking about her. About their goodbye and that last kiss she'd pressed against his lips. The way his fists had clenched as he'd forced his hands to still rather than pull her against him.

She was supposed to be out of his head by now.

Maybe it was the sex he was missing. Though there were more than enough willing women lurking around the hotel lobby and bar, casting inviting looks. But he wasn't interested in the slightest. He didn't want to buy them a drink. Didn't want to waste a few hours on idle conversation. Or try to forget for a few minutes in their arms. Nothing interested him. No one.

He wondered if Cali had been able to figure a workaround on the pricing delay that had cropped up before he left. Wondered if she'd been pushing herself too hard, staying up all night to resolve the problem. Staying too late at the office alone. Taking cabs in the middle of the night. His gut tightened as his fingers wrapped around the phone in his pocket.

He just wanted to know she was okay. A fling didn't necessitate a complete lack of feelings. Of course he cared about her. He had from the start. Which was why he was leaving her alone.

He was being an idiot. Still, he stared down at the phone, debating a moment longer, before shoving it back into his pocket and heading to the table where his partner was talking to another group of surgeons.

Cali was exhausted. At the office, she'd been a dynamo. Pushing everyone around her, demanding progress, inciting action. She'd been going full throttle, trying to keep her attention on the task at hand rather than on the persistent ache inside her. But when the building was locked up for the night, and she was forced to go home, sleep would not come. All she could do was stare at the ceiling, blinking eyes she refused to let cry, fighting the pain she'd been too stupid to avoid.

Four days had passed since Jake had returned from the conference. She'd seen him once, hailing a cab just as she'd arrived—nearly called and run over before catching herself at the last minute.

Breaking things off was the right thing to do. She'd needed to refocus on her career. Stop investing so much energy and emotion in a relationship that wasn't going anywhere. So she kept telling herself the same things, time and again. It was for the best. It was time to let go. Only the hollow sensation deep inside her wasn't lessening. She missed his body, missed the way he made her feel. She missed more than that, but thinking about exactly how much she'd lost hurt more than she could bear.

Fatigue pressed heavy on her shoulders as she pushed with her hip through the revolving lobby doors. She was suddenly so tired it was all she could do not to rest her forehead against the glass. Maybe her mind would stop spinning and she'd finally sleep tonight.

* * *

There she was, mere yards ahead of him. Fine—now he'd seen her. He'd been telling himself for days the reason he couldn't get her out of his head was that he hadn't seen her yet. But as he'd stepped out of the Snappy Store and caught a glimpse of her heading into their building, half a block away, no sense of closure had come to him. He didn't want to stand where he was and wait for her to catch the elevator without him. Didn't feel relieved or released or anything but an impossible to ignore urge to go to her. Talk to her. Make sure she was okay.

Fists balled at his sides, he willed his feet to stay where they were, but every muscle in his body began to rebel against the rationale of his mind.

Crossing the lobby, Cali cursed the gorgeous three-inch heels she'd put on that morning, thinking they were comfortable. They were sprint distance shoes—showy—not suited for the long haul. At the end of the road, with the elevators off to the next alcove, each step sent a stab of pain from her toes to her calf.

Only a few more steps and she'd be able to shut down. Relax.

She pushed the up button just as a familiar, baritone voice called her name, starting a chain reaction of awareness surging through her body.

No. Not now. Not when her every reserve was exhausted.

Jake. Dressed in a charcoal suit, white shirt, and slate tie. His trench coat flared behind him as he strode across the open lobby. He looked harder, more impenetrable than she'd ever seen him, his flinty gaze steady on her as his steps ate up the distance between them.

Her nails dug into her palms as a warm tide of longing washed through her veins. "Welcome back, Jake."

"Thanks." He stopped beside her, leaning one shoulder

against the wall, his hands stuffed deep in his trouser pockets. Casual. Polite. Easy, damn him. "So, I'm guessing these are the spy hours you were talking about, huh?"

Answering with a weak smile and a nod, she stared straight ahead. She couldn't look at him. Couldn't let him see what his presence alone did to her.

"How've you been?" So very adult. Polite.

"Busy," she answered evasively. "You know."

"Sure." Jake let out a long breath beside her, and when he spoke again irritation edged his words. "Thought I would have seen you before this. You've been working late a lot."

Had he been looking? No. He hadn't phoned, and for heaven's sake the man lived on the other side of her wall. If he'd wanted to see her, he would have.

The elevator doors opened and she glanced at the small space within, then gazed longingly at the stairwell opposite where they stood. She could walk up. Avoid that brief confinement with Jake altogether.

What were seventeen floors, anyway?

Who was she kidding? The cruel shoes wouldn't make it to the second landing, and, more to the point, Jake wasn't the kind of man to let her march off like that if he had something to say. Or hobble off, as the case may be.

The image was too pathetic, and she sighed with resignation as she stepped into the waiting car. It was seventeen floors. What could happen?

"Did you do anything this weekend?" he asked, watching her from the corner.

"Just worked, really." She'd passed on making plans with Trish. Turned down a date from one of the accounting guys. Just given herself over to the job for as many hours as it would take her.

"Of course. Get far enough ahead to feel like you aren't behind yet?"

She laughed at that, almost turned to look at him, before quickly turning back to stare at the passing floors illuminate and dim, the smile dying on her lips.

"That laugh. You don't know how good it is to hear it after…." A low hiss of strained breath filled the silence, followed by a rough curse that had her head snapping around in alarm.

"Jake?" Peering up into the deep blue eyes that searched her soul, she noted a weariness. Something almost haunted just beneath the surface. "Are you okay?"

Jake pulled back, as though shocked by the question. Stunned that he'd revealed anything at all. His looked away, but only for a second, before he was back in control.

The elevator chimed and the doors slid open. Cali dragged her gaze from the man she simply wanted to hold. Turned to the hall and forced her feet to move.

It's for the best. She could let—

"I miss you."

She froze in place. Closed her eyes—shook her head the slightest degree. She couldn't breathe. Didn't want to dare hope.

"I thought it would go away, this thing between us. But I'm watching you walk down this hall without me…and I don't want to let you go."

He was beside her now, not touching, but close enough for the heat of his body to warm her, his breath to tease her hair. "Cali."

Tension arced between them, the air almost vibrating with it. Another inch and there'd be contact, and then it would be too late. Her arms would be around his neck, her body hot against his. She wouldn't be able to resist. Wouldn't want to—

His arms closed around her, his lips descending in a brutal crush. She opened, groaning at the taste of him in her mouth.

The tight grip of his hands in her clothes. So good. So right. She needed more.

He gathered her tightly into his embrace. Lifting her feet from the ground, he walked them, mouths fused, tongues sliding over and around each other, down the hall. She registered the door to his apartment as they moved past and then stopped at hers.

Distance.

Insurance that he'd be able to leave.

Nothing had changed. Not really. Because even though he'd missed her...*he hadn't wanted to.*

Like her, he simply couldn't resist. Eyes closed, she savored the strength of the body against hers—the warmth and scent. She wanted this. Needed it. Had tried going without and nothing about it felt right. So she would have a part of him, but not all—less than she wanted, but more than she'd hoped for. It was physical rather than emotional, and if she could remember that—keep a part of her heart guarded because of it—she could live with it...if he could.

"Jake," she breathed against his lips, her fingers clenched in the fabric of his shirt, her body melting in a slow glide against the contours of his frame. "Is this really what you want?"

He stopped, chest heaving, muscles bunched. He wanted her more than his next breath. How could she even ask when just exactly *how much he wanted her* was stabbing her in the belly.

But sex wasn't what she meant.

Did he even know what he wanted? All he knew was that nothing made sense and everything felt off. His skin didn't fit. He couldn't breathe right. The rhythm of his existence was out of sync. But, standing so close to Cali, he felt the pull of a gravitational slide bringing him ever closer. He stared into her eyes. Down to her kiss-swollen lips as she whispered his name. Saw her sitting there at the Jazz House that very first night; snapping her chopsticks at him, laughing, as they dined on her floor; falling asleep with her lips pressed at the center of his chest.

And then he knew.

He couldn't keep fighting her. Didn't want to try.

Screw the strings. The messy complications. The future. All the reasons he'd used to keep a distance between them that was driving him insane.

His fingers sifted into her curls as he coaxed her head back. Their eyes met. Held. "All I want is you."

She blinked, looked closer, as if she couldn't believe what he'd said or what she saw. When she answered, her voice had gone rough with emotion, her eyes dark with need. "God, I've missed you."

He bowed down and, finding her lips open and waiting, welcoming to the thrust of his tongue, swept her into his arms. The weight of her in his hold, her soft, eager kiss, the gentle pressure of her fingers grasping and releasing at his shoulders as he carried her back to her room were sustenance to his starving soul. A balm to his battered heart.

He needed her. All of her.

Setting her to her feet within the bedroom, he broke from their kiss. Pressed his brow against hers and closed his eyes. Less than two weeks had passed since he'd last entered this space that acted as sanctuary to the woman in his arms, but tonight it felt as though he'd been away forever. Too damn long, and his own damn fault.

No more.

Hands moving to the buttons of her blouse, he parted the silk panels by increments until they hung free and finally slipped to the floor. She was beautiful standing there, staring up at him with those soulful green eyes, her fingers trembling as they worked the buttons of his shirt.

Silently, slowly, they removed each other's clothing until

they both stood naked, breath coming ragged between them. But he wouldn't rush. No matter how much a part of him wanted to toss her to the bed and drive himself deep within her as fast he could, a greater part of him needed more. Needed to feel the heat of her skin against his own, the beating of her heart, the delicate frame of her within his hold. Needed all that was Cali. All he'd been missing.

Her fingers skimmed light over his chest, shoulders, neck, and then up to his jaw. A butterfly touch—too tentative and yet perfect. Peering up at him, she whispered, "I need you, Jake."

A ragged groan escaped him as he buried his nose in the curls tumbling over her shoulder, held her tight against him. "Sweetheart, you don't even know."

Cali lay back upon the bed then, all pure, bare, soft skin, stretched out beneath him as he covered her with his body. With urgency a torrent through his veins, hard to the point of pain, he settled in the cradle of her hips.

"Cali," he gritted out, wanting to explain—to give her something—only no words would come. How could he explain what he didn't understand himself? All he knew was that the sensible, reasonable solution had made him miserable, and now he simply could not be without her for another day.

She shook her head, lips parting to take his kiss, arms circling his neck to draw him down to her.

He drew back, notching the wide head of himself at her opening. Then nudged forward, his teeth clenched through the exquisite agony of his overcharged nerves, penetrating the body he'd gone too long without.

Sweet, sweet Cali. She was heaven. Salvation. Decadent and essential all at once, gasping her pleasure as she took him within her.

Her lips pressed at the hollow in the center of his chest, so soft breath caressed his throat with whispers and sighs that heightened his every sense, drove his need to near desperation.

Her body arched as he pushed into the snug clasp of her, burying himself to the hilt, reaching…reaching…seeking a closeness, a union he couldn't quite fathom, but sensed just beyond his grasp.

A thin sheen of sweat covered their skin, slicking the glide of flesh against flesh. He was lost in the rhythmic thrust and retreat, the hungry kiss of her body as his groin brushed hers with one intimate caress after another, the breathy, satisfied sounds she made at the nudging of her womb with his every stroke.

Cali's soft pleas came steadily, her body translating the broken mindless words that fell from her lips.

More…. Like that…. Again….

She was close, and every part of his being focused on taking her there. Making her feel good.

Seeking the erect tip of her nipple, he drew it into his mouth, alternating suction with teasing licks, each pull driving her cries and answering spasms higher. His teeth closed over the tight bud, and with the point of his tongue he pushed the tender peak against the roof of his mouth.

"Oh, Jake…."

He felt her keening response in every point of contact between them. She seized harder with every thrust and lick of flesh. Clutched tighter with each retreat, until he couldn't take it any longer. He withdrew slowly, and as he sank deep again rocked his groin, trapping her clitoris between their bodies.

His lips lowered to her ear, brushing the outer shell with his words. "Cali… Cali… Cali…let go, baby."

Her hands clutched against him, she arched back, her body constricting time and again. Swallowing her sweet cries with his kiss, he felt tension gather at the base of his spine. Sensation pulled inward, pulsing hot through his body toward one central spot.

This was what he needed. Wanted. Had waited for. The reason he couldn't eat, sleep, or breathe without thinking of her. Because he needed *this*.

To connect.

Join.

Hold.

Possess.

His mind was blanked of anything beyond his body merging with hers, again and again, until one coherent thought rose above the rush of his blood past his ears.

Mine. Mine. Mine.

He let go. The restraint he'd clung to so ferociously shattered under the hammering of his hips. He roared, body quaking, lungs burning with his release into the silky hold of her body.

Forehead resting in the crook of Cali's neck, his body still lodged within her, Jake felt the racing beat of her heart, the heat rising off her skin, the lingering ripples of her climax. It was satisfaction of the purest and most complete variety. Relief so deep it permeated every cell of his being. It was the restoration of peace of mind… Bliss… Oblivion.

A persistent beeping and the tickle of soft curls slipping over his shoulder woke him. Cali groaned, knocking the alarm to the floor, and then dropped back beside him, arms tucked up against her chest.

Tuesday morning, sometime. Knowing the way she worked, he couldn't even guess when. "What time is it?"

"Five," she answered, stretching long, with one hand fisted high above her head. "I fell asleep without resetting the alarm and…and I didn't know you'd still be here."

He ran his palm over the rough stubble of his jaw, propped himself on an elbow to face her. "Sorry I am?"

"No," she answered hesitantly, her focus on the sheet between them, where she traced little circles with her index finger. "But I thought sleepovers were against the rules."

He nodded his acknowledgment at that. But the truth was he'd been breaking his rules since the minute he'd met her—the only time things hadn't worked was when he'd stopped. And being without her had been hell. "Maybe we should forget about the rules."

The hint of a smile played at the corner of her lips as her gaze lifted to his. "Really?"

"Yeah. You won't be here forever, but while you are…. Let's see what happens if we just do what feels good."

An impish glint lit her eyes as she shifted closer, bringing her naked lower body into contact with his. "You mean drop out of society because we never leave this bed again?"

He flipped her onto her back, pinning her down with his body. "Or maybe something less drastic. We can break to order food delivery."

"Keep your strength up? Smart." Her knee skimmed up his side, higher and higher still, until her lower leg snaked across his butt. "You're going to need it."

How the hell had he thought he could let her go?

CHAPTER SIXTEEN

CALI set down her sandwich and brushed a few stray crumbs with the side of her hand. "Okay, I think we're good."

Across the report-littered desk, Trish considered her top page of notes, tapping her pen against each bulleted item. "Yep. I'll get onto Neal about pulling in his date. You handle Carl." Then, slumping back in her chair, she grabbed her soda cup and took a sip. "We're going to get ulcers, working through lunch like this every day."

Cali shook her head. "That's slacker propaganda. I'd get an ulcer if I tried to eat with so much left to be done." Besides, working lunches and early starts left more time free in the evenings for her other activities.

Trish shook her head. "Look at that grin on you! You're a sick puppy. You know that, right?"

It was potentially true, but Cali waved her off with a laugh. "Like you're any better!"

Trish was still picking at her chips, taking a minute to relax before jumping back into the fray. "So, this isn't the first borderline obnoxiously wide smile I've seen stretched across your face this week. In fact, I'd say they're becoming something of a standard with you these days. Dish it up, Cali. Where'd he take you this week?"

"We went to the symphony one night. But we've… umm…been getting a lot of take-out." This time Cali had to look away. Trish didn't need to know just exactly how close to reality her hedonistic fantasy had become. They ordered in, ate in bed, ate on the floor… Once, Jake had even eaten his dessert off her.

Heat surged her system at the memory of cold, wet ice cream contrasting with the heat of his mouth—

Oh, God, Trish was still there. Crinkling her nose with disapproval as she studied her nails. "That's it? I thought Dr. Romance was all about the trendy Chicago hotspots. I'm bored."

Cali rolled her eyes, thankful her friend's distraction by her manicure had kept her from catching on to just how *not boring* an evening at home with Jake was. They talked forever. Laughed so much she thought she'd have a washboard stomach from it before the month was through. And then, at the end of the night, he just held her. Ran his hand over her back, fiddled with her hair…and fell asleep with his arms wrapped tight around her.

"Wow," Trish interrupted with a raised brow. "That sigh sounds serious."

Cali felt the heat washing over her skin at the thoughts and feelings that had come in to her head. What could she say without giving herself away?

"O… M… G! I *knew* it! Chicago is *so* going to be your favorite city. Every time you see a movie filmed here, or have to coordinate with this office, you're going to get that faraway look in your eye, remembering your lusty affair in the Windy City. *So romantic*," Trish gushed, completely wrapped up in her fantasy—until she noticed Cali had frozen in place. Brow furrowing, she flattened her hands on the desktop, as if to steady them both. "Wait. You *are* still planning to go, aren't you? London's still calling, right? Cali? My career girl idol, please tell me you aren't considering selling everything you've worked for short for some stud in a white coat."

Cali laughed, shaking her head as if she was shaking off nonsense.

Only Trish wasn't buying. "Cali, you've been busting that backside of yours for years. Priorities, girl!"

"I know. And I'm not giving anything up. I just haven't spent a lot of time thinking about what's happening next." Until Trish had verbalized a scenario she didn't want to contemplate, she hadn't *let* herself think about it, for once focusing on the now rather than the end goal. She'd been taking each day, each night, as it came. Falling into Jake's arms, falling into his bed, falling into something deeper than she'd thought possible. But, no matter how good things seemed with Jake, she knew better than to assume it meant anything had really changed. Only knowing hadn't stopped her from wishing. "I mean, Amanda still hasn't given me my next assignment. For all I know, it could be here."

"Or it could be in London," Trish said, all trace of joking gone.

"Yes. Or it could be London," she conceded, with less optimism than the statement merited.

Trish's features hardened into a stern mask. "A month ago you wouldn't have even—" She looked away, blowing out an exasperated breath before looking back. "Does he even *love* you?"

Cali stared back at her, shoulders stiffening. "That's none of your business, Trish."

"Okay, fine. You're right. Our friendship didn't grow out of feminine confidences and broken hearts. It grew out of a mutual desire to kick corporate ass. We've been cheering each other on, offering advice and support, for years. So how about this? I suggest you figure out if this guy loves you before your sudden ambivalence re your career has you toasting someone else's departure to Heathrow."

"Trish—"

But she was already walking through the door, a hand waving over her shoulder. "Yeah, yeah. You know it's because I care. I know we're still friends."

Cali went to the window, pressed her forehead against the glass and stared out at the cityscape beyond. This job was important to her. It had been the only important thing for too many years to suddenly have second thoughts when she was so close to achieving her goal. Of course *second thoughts* hadn't exactly been the issue. More like avoidance altogether.

The last two weeks with Jake had been incredible. Everything she'd never even thought to hope for and more. His caring was obvious, demonstrated in a million little ways…but, as intense as what they had seemed to be, it was still new. Topics like the future were glossed over in only the most general way. Sure, he'd mentioned things she'd love to see—like the evening drive into the city at the height of fall, and fat flakes swirling past the rough-hewn stones of the old Water Tower during a new snow. Things he knew she wouldn't be around to see unless she stayed.

Why was she even thinking about this? London was her dream. What she had to do for *herself*.

But the way he made her feel when he let his guard down…there was nothing like it. It was the kind of feeling that made a career girl rethink her commitments to herself.

There was only one problem.

A part of her wondered if the only reason Jake could be so wonderful, so open, was because he knew she was leaving. She didn't want to believe it, but this man was commitment-averse in ways she could only begin to fathom, but already knew to fear.

Before the incident with Pam she would never have believed what had happened afterward possible. Even now it seemed unreal. Impossible that Jake was the same man. But he was. Which, when she allowed herself to think about it, made the fact that she'd fallen so helplessly, completely in love with him all the more terrifying.

Jake cracked another egg against the glass rim of his bowl and tossed the shell into the sink. After wiping his hand on the dishtowel slung over his shoulder, he scooped up the mound of grated white cheddar and sliced spring onions, then whisked them into the eggs with a fork.

A little seasoning, and into the skillet for a scramble. Pushing the eggs around, he watched them firm and fluff until they were done.

He caught movement from the corner of his eye and turned to find Cali, leaning against the door frame, wrapped in the Oxford shirt he'd worn the night before. Her eyes were puffy from sleep, and her cheek still held a crease from her pillow, but she was so sexy.

"Morning, beautiful."

Her mouth twisted into a scowl as she shook her head at him. "You need to get your eyes checked. I can't believe I slept so late. How long have you been up?"

Two slices of multigrain popped from the toaster and Jake dropped them onto plates, smearing a dollop of marmalade across the golden top of each. "An hour?"

Cali yawned, stretching up on her toes with one arm over her head. Panties. No bra. And two little buttons doing a poor job of keeping her decent in front of a man with very indecent ideas.

A glob of marmalade slithered down his thumb from the spoon he held frozen in midair. She got to him. He'd seen her like this every morning, and usually a few times throughout the night, and yet a teasing glimpse of the lower curve of her breast, or the sliver of flesh exposed by the gap at the bottom of his shirt held him transfixed, body stirring, brain plotting the quickest way to get her wrapped around him again.

His gut clenched every time he thought about how close he'd come to losing her—throwing her away. He'd been an idiot of epic proportions. But no more.

And only an idiot wouldn't take advantage of the sexy little sweetheart gift wrapped in a half-open Oxford in front of him.

Cali glanced up, sensing the change in the air, the thickening tension. Jake stood, propped against the counter by the sink, looking insanely sexy, with worn jeans riding low on his hips and nothing more than a dishtowel draped over his shoulder on top.

"Come here." The cocky smile spread over his sensuous lips had her heart skipping in her chest and awareness surging hot through her veins. She stepped into the muscular cradle of one extended arm. Jake licked the sticky bit of marmalade from his thumb and leaned down to kiss her, slipping his tongue into her mouth for a shared taste of seduction.

"Mmm, sweet," she whispered as he pulled back to lick at the corner of her mouth. His hands moved to her hips, and in one swift motion he'd set her on the counter in front of him.

Desire lanced her core. One kiss and she was aching for him.

Her phone rattled against the counter behind her, Amanda's text message alert pinging in the background. Cali pushed her fingers into Jake's hair, pulling his mouth down to hers for another taste of him.

"Don't you need to get that?" he asked, his wicked smile brushing her lips.

"Later," she whispered. "It's Saturday."

Jake pulled away with a scolding *tsk*. "Yeah, like that'll

stop you. Read it. You'll think about it—no matter how distracting my efforts—until you've checked it."

At that moment nothing seemed as important to her as sating their need to join together, but what Jake was saying *should* be right. She grabbed for the phone, trying to ignore the unsettling knowledge that this was the second time in so many days someone else had stepped in to keep her on point.

Her focus locked on the small screen in her hand, where tiny letters were strung together, making up the words she'd been waiting to read. She blinked, blinked again, feeling her vision tunnel, her heart accelerate and her stomach plunge.

Jake nudged his hips between her legs, his smile glinting in her periphery. Fingers splayed over her bare thighs, thumbs lightly circling her inner flesh. "What's up?"

She peered at him, too many conflicting emotions overwhelming her at once. Too many questions taking on an urgency she hadn't acknowledged until this instant. Suddenly she wished she'd left the message unread—given herself a few more minutes in Jake's arms to soak in the contentment and peace of a simple Saturday morning—because now everything had changed.

"I'm going to London." The words were past her lips, riding the air between them, before she thought to consider her phrasing. It wasn't a question or a possibility she'd put forth, it was a statement of fact—a subconscious dare or plea to the man in front of her to shake his head tell her no. Give her a clue as to how he felt about her leaving.

Only shock had wiped all expression from his face, leaving it blank for the space of a heartbeat. All it took for him to regain control and pull his features into a mask of composure. "Congratulations, Cali." He stepped back, crossed his arms over his chest. "I never doubted you'd get it."

So that was that. Okay. At least she knew.

"Thank you," she answered, managing a thin smile through the welling hurt as she slipped off the counter. "There's a meeting in an hour to discuss the details. I need to shower and get ready." Spend a few minutes with her own thoughts, trying to sort out her emotions. Get herself to a place where she could be happy.

She took a step toward the hall, but Jake caught her wrist. She turned, hope burning through her like a flash flame at his touch.

"Breakfast, sweetheart." He stuffed a wedge of toast between her lips and ducked to drop a kiss at her temple. "A few bites'll keep you sharp for the meeting. And then we'll celebrate tonight, with dinner someplace special."

She stared for a second, until Jake let out a short laugh, spun her around and sent her off with a light swat on her derrière. "Get moving, sweetheart. London awaits."

London awaits, she thought heading down the hall on feet she couldn't feel, chewing toast she couldn't taste, preparing to celebrate a victory she couldn't enjoy.

No. Couldn't enjoy *yet*.

She was numb from the shock, was all. London was everything she'd wanted. Everything she'd been working for. Years of hard work and effort paying off. And Jake supported her in that. Understood how much it meant to her.

She was lucky. There weren't any tough choices ahead of her. No questions that needed answering after all.

Lucky. Lucky. Lucky.

Bathed in the soundless blue glow of a late-night movie, Jake reclined against the headboard, absently stroking Cali's tumble of wild curls as she slept against his chest.

His hand moved over the dark cherry and ginger waves, his fingers sifting into the soft disarray. She snuggled closer, her breath and lips tickling his abdomen with unintelligible murmurings.

Talking in her sleep again.

Usually it was just a few words, if that. Sometimes she said his name. He could gauge the quality of her dreaming based on the sounds that followed. A breathless laugh. A languorous moan. Being the ego-driven ass that he was, the moan was his favorite, and he rarely suppressed the answering urge to wake her and make the dream reality.

Tonight he found himself listening closely, willing his heartbeat to quiet as he tried to decipher her words. What he was listening for he didn't know. Answers to questions he hadn't asked, maybe?

Ten days. They were pulling her out of Chicago in ten days. Not even letting her finish the project here. She'd gotten far enough ahead that they'd decided to bring in someone else to tie up the rest, so Cali could get started in London.

She was getting what she wanted.

They both were.

He'd known from the start Chicago was nothing more than a stepping stone in the path of Cali's career, and it was that very lack of permanence which had allowed him to give in and relax with her the way he had. But, even knowing it was coming, he'd received the news of her assignment with a disturbing mix of relief and distress. And so soon? He'd thought he had close to a month, but she'd come back from the meeting that had run well into the afternoon with a stunned expression, sixteen pages of notes, and a time frame of ten days.

He felt cheated. Angry just *anticipating* waking a few short days from now without her stretched beside him, all rumpled and warm.

When he came home at night there would be no one to

meet him with little stories or silly jokes or soft kisses or quiet company.

He'd date. An endless series of superficial, short-lived encounters that never would have seemed hollow before Cali gave him something to compare them to.

It had been years since the solitude of living alone had even registered with him. When Pam had left, sure, it had been hard. His marriage might not have been the romance legends were made of, but for more years than not Pam had been his friend. He'd liked sharing a life with her—until he'd discovered she'd been sharing it with someone else as well. But being alone after that companionable existence—it had taken time and some drastic measures to fall back into the comfort of bachelor living.

Measures like the obnoxious TV, mounted sports-bar-style in the living room. The exercise equipment side by side with his couch. The steady stream of take-out dinners and take-out sex. And it had worked. He'd adapted to his new lifestyle so completely that once he'd found his groove he'd spent years avoiding anything—anyone—with the potential to disrupt it.

Until Cali. Everything was different with her, and had been from almost the first minute he'd met her.

He'd been looking for ways to have her that didn't conform to the mold of his life. Thinking that because she was *supposed* to leave he'd be able to have his cake and eat it too. Enjoy that forbidden comfort of emotional and physical intimacy blending together as day chased night round and again. Thinking he'd be able to let her go simply because it had been the plan from the start.

Only he already knew what it felt like to be without her.

Fisting his hands against his eyes, he let his head fall back against the pillows.

Everything was playing out just as it should, except now

he didn't want it to go this way. Suddenly her impending departure didn't feel like the free pass he'd once thought it to be. He didn't want her to leave.

His breath held.

Was he actually considering this?

A soft sigh feathered over his navel, tightening every muscle in his body.

Hell, yes, he was.

"Cali." He pushed her hair from her eyes and stroked her shoulder before he could come up with a reason not to. "Wake up, sweetheart."

"Hmm?" She shifted against his chest, resting on her chin to face him. "You okay?"

"Do you ever think about picking a city to settle in?"

A tiny furrow drew between her eyes as they blinked in confusion. "What?"

What did she see? Some jackass leering at her with a phony smile? What had happened to the man who'd made her moan in the phone booth of a bar?

"Chicago. Staying here. With me." There'd been a hesitance in her eyes when she'd gotten the news. He'd seen it, made sure he didn't offer even one thing to feed into it. But now that felt like a mistake.

She pushed up from his chest, but he took her arms and laid her back on the pillow, then braced himself on one elbow beside her.

The sleepy fog cleared from her gaze as she focused on him. "What are you asking me, Jake?"

His hand slipped beneath the sheet to cover the smooth, soft plane of her belly, where he traced light patterns over her skin. "We make each other happy. What we've got feels good—too good to let it end when it's barely just begun."

Cali blinked owl-wide eyes at him. This was a subject carefully avoided up to this point. He could feel the tension coiling within her. "What does that mean? Are you asking me to—?"

No.

"I'm asking you to stay, see how this thing between us plays out." He took her hand, stroking his thumb over her knuckles. "I know your plan's been to go international, but is it so important to go now? Come on, Cali. You feel it too— we haven't run our course yet."

The long muscles of her throat worked as she swallowed. She sat up and scooted back, blocking the emotion in her eyes as she slipped from his grasp to leave his hand on the cooling sheet where she'd been. She tugged the edge of the comforter up around her breasts and held it there, her body language conveying the words she seemed to struggle to voice. "I'm committed to this assignment."

People changed their minds all the time. "The job hasn't started yet. MetroTrek will find someone else."

Cali froze, the skin tightening across her body as another man's words rang through her mind. *"It's just a job, baby. They can get someone else."*

She shook it off and took a deep breath before returning his gaze. Jake wasn't Erik. This wasn't the same. Not really. Erik was a selfish bastard. A liar.

Jake wasn't. But what he'd offered her—a chance to let the relationship run its course—wasn't enough. Not even close. And it had taken everything in her not to wince from the hurt of such a limited offer. "I have goals, *plans for myself.*"

"I know you do, but there's such a thing as compromise. Some of those goals could be met here," he urged. "You'll transfer within the company."

Cali stared up into the deep blue of Jake's eyes, where his emotions played a peek-a-boo game in the flickering light of the television. Arguing with him was the last thing she wanted to do. She reached out to touch the line of his jaw, felt the muscle jump beneath her palm. It wasn't supposed to be like this. He was supposed to tell her he loved her. Give her something solid to hold onto. Not this half-promise to let their relationship "play out". To try for London some other time. She'd done that once already…and it had led her right back here. This time she owed it to herself to follow through.

Her stomach twisted anxiously as she opened her mouth, but Jake put a finger to her lips, shook his head. "I shouldn't have started this tonight. Neither of us are thinking clearly. Let's get some sleep and talk about it tomorrow."

He eased down into the pillows, pulling her with him. Emotion clogged her throat as the circle of his arms tightened and his lips pressed at the top of her head. There was no denying how good it felt to be in his arms. Just like there was no denying that Cali had nearly thrown her career away once before, gambling on a relationship without a future. And, no matter what Jake said the next day, she couldn't let herself do it again.

CHAPTER SEVENTEEN

MOUNTED on the outer rail surrounding the rooftop deck, lamps flickered and glowed in molten hues against the darkening sky. A perimeter of flames danced in the rising wind, illuminating the MetroTrek crowd gathered at a co-worker's Bucktown loft condo to bid Cali farewell. It was Friday night, and she was booked on the eight-fifteen, flying out Saturday evening.

Rubbing her arms against the evening chill made worse by the incoming weather, Cali watched the crowd at the bar laugh at something Jake said, while a strawberry-blonde threw her head back and then pressed her chest forward, gripping his arm for support. Jake gave her hand a quick pat and then gently extracted himself from her hold, turning back to Matt.

Women wanted him. All the time, it seemed. Everywhere they went hair swung in provocative fans, beckoning him closer. She knew he noticed, was probably so used to it he simply expected it. He certainly hadn't been flustered any of the times he'd called *her* out for so blatantly gobbling up an eyeful of his good looks.

He wouldn't be alone for long once she left. Not even one night—not unless he wanted to be.

A dull ache rose in her chest as she wondered if that was how he would deal with her leaving. The idea of his hands on another woman killed her.

Unreasonable. She knew it. Tried to tamp down the cacophony of emotions rattling her every nerve, shaking her confidence. Her faith.

What was she doing?

Jake pushed a wayward hank of his dark hair back from his brow and glanced up from his conversation with Matt. Their eyes met. From across the space of a building she felt his stare run hot over her cool skin, sparking the smolder of lust low in her belly. Her bar-side savior. Tall, dark, and more devastating to her heart than she'd ever believed possible.

Only one more night.

Oh, God, this hurt. She quickly looked away, trying to hide the pain in her eyes, but Jake was already crossing the deck. Within seconds his hand had closed over her hip, and he'd pulled her into the warmth of his chest.

"Look at me, Cali," he rasped, somehow making it both a plea and a command.

Her eyes met his. Soulful blue stared back at her, and the first tear slipped from the corner of her eye. Stupid. She shouldn't have let him see. Shouldn't have given him another opening to start a conversation that had to end the same way.

Jake's hold tightened, the muscle in his jaw jumping with strain in his face. "Don't go. I can see you hurting, but you don't have to. Just don't go."

He didn't understand. Maybe he didn't even want to. She loved him, but she would never forgive herself if she didn't leave. "Please—"

"You've turned this job into something it shouldn't be. London is just another city. It's not your whole life. You could have success here. Hell, Cali, I'll set you up with your own firm if that would make you happy. I'll give you any kind of business you want. I don't care if you work at all. Volunteer. Quit altogether and take up yoga."

She blinked, stunned and confused, trying not to laugh. "You're trying to set me up as your kept mistress? Do I get my own town house and a yearly income too?"

But for once Jake didn't share her humor. He shook his head, staring at the sky as he gritted out words she was certain he wanted to yell. "There are other solutions than running a quarter of the way around the globe to make a point just because I won't—"

She waited, knowing he wouldn't say the words. *Love her.*

She should have been used to it by now, but somehow every time she had to register why she needed to leave it was harder to face than the last. As if she kept expecting at any minute he would see reason and realize he loved her.

"Don't do this now," she pleaded. Pulling herself free, she turned away from him, dragging the breath into her lungs.

"Then when, Cali? You've been working from six in the morning until ten at night for the last week. You're leaving tomorrow and we're spending our last hours together with a bunch of your co-workers who look like they're more excited about getting liquored up than they are about you actually going to London. You can't put me off any longer. We need to talk."

One hour later they were home. Cali watched as rain pelted the windows of her mostly packed apartment, hammering home the fact that her existence in Chicago had nearly been washed away. Jake stood behind her, more ominous than the thunder rolling across the blackened sky.

"You won't even commit to a visit."

She turned on him, demanding understanding. "All I asked

was that we wait to see how you feel after I've been gone for a while before making those kinds of plans."

"See how I feel? I'm the one who's telling you not to go! I think it's pretty damn clear how I feel."

She couldn't keep going round with him this way. Her head was spinning, heart aching, and all she wanted to do was spend the next dozen hours soaking up the feeling of Jake's arms around her. They weren't getting anywhere, but he wouldn't let it go. "You feel that way now, but once I'm gone—"

"So don't go! Don't give me the chance to forget about you if that's what you're so sure is going to happen."

"Right!" she lashed back, unable to stop the words spewing from her mouth. "So I give up everything I've been working for, *for years*, and then what happens the next time Pam drops out of the sky with some crisis and you're suddenly reminded of your commitment issues? The next time you decide you don't like what you see in my eyes? That I've overstepped the bounds of our relationship?" She should have stopped, but he'd pushed her, refused to let it go, and now something inside her wouldn't allow this to remain unsaid. "There's one thing I can't forget, no matter how much I'd like to, Jake. You might not have been able to let me go…but you *wanted to*."

They both stilled. Cali held her breath. Waited for the impact to dull, the words to dissipate into nothing. Only they hung heavy around them, pushing against the backs of her eyes, tightening her throat, weighing on her soul.

She couldn't even say his name. Try to take it back. Her voice would crack; her tears would spill.

His hands slid over her shoulders, up her neck to cup her jaw in his palms as he rested his brow against hers. "Cali…."

"I can't fight with you." Couldn't he understand? "I can't bear for things to end like this."

"Okay. I know. You're going." Jake's gaze, as dark and stormy as the night raging beyond the glass, slid over her. There was hurt there. And acceptance. "Just give me tonight. We'll end it right."

CHAPTER EIGHTEEN

"THIS isn't going to cut it, Marcus. I need the forecast revised to include all of these factors." Cali turned back to face her computer before he cleared away from her desk, and didn't bother to watch him close the door behind him. The guy had been pushing her buttons since she'd arrived in London. He was getting careless with his work and becoming a liability to the project. She'd need to make a decision about him quickly.

Her desk phone sounded and she reached for it on the first ring. "Calista McGovern."

"Amanda, here. What've you got for me?"

Cali closed her eyes while she rattled off the projections, numbers and status updates to her boss, forcing her concentration to the business at hand and away from Dr. Jake Tyler, whom it drifted toward without more than the slightest provocation.

Pretty much every call, text, e-mail or report with Amanda's name on it sent Cali into an emotional free fall. And that was while she was buried alive with work to distract her. At home— Well, she spent more than her fair share of time contemplating what she'd done. What he might be doing. What might have been.

It had been two weeks since she'd left Chicago—two weeks since she'd kissed him, felt his warmth around her, drawn in the heady scent of his body—two weeks since this ceaseless ache had taken root in the center of her heart.

She'd made the right choice in leaving. Had to believe it, because giving in to even an instant's doubt was more pain than she could bear. But the distance, the loss, wasn't getting any easier.

Amanda's voice brought her back to the task at hand. "You're ahead of schedule, then. I knew you'd be able to handle the job."

"Thank you. I appreciate your confidence."

Her boss hesitated, then asked, "Have you spoken to Jackson?"

Jake. In her heart, he'd always be hers.

Cali slumped in her chair, hating the tightening of her throat and the tears that threatened to well in her eyes. "No. I left him a message to let him know I'd arrived." She swallowed past the rising knot of emotion, took a deep breath. "Clean break and all that. It's probably better this way."

"He won't talk to me about you. I worry— Well, never mind. How is London working out for you?"

Cali immediately pulled out the top report from the clutter of her desk. "You've seen the numbers—"

"No, I mean aside from the job. After you leave the office. The life part."

Cali actually pulled the phone from her ear, staring dumbly at the receiver as though it could answer this question for her. There *was* no life.

Amanda's voice was quiet as it came back over the line. "Have you thought at all about going back to Chicago?"

Pretty much since the minute she'd left. But what she'd had with Jake— If he couldn't love her, the imbalance of their relationship would be too hard to bear. "I loved it there, but it probably wouldn't be a good idea."

Another sigh from across the ocean. "Well, if you change your mind there's a permanent position opening under Aaron Lansing. I think you'd be an excellent candidate. And, before you ask, this has nothing to do with Jake. It's just that eventually people in your position find a location they fall in love with and then find a way to stay there. Think about it."

She *had* fallen in love with Chicago. And if she hadn't fallen in love with Jake, then maybe. Only she had. "Thank you, Amanda. I'll keep it in mind."

A month had passed since Cali arrived in London, and almost as long since she'd realized she would never be a true Londoner. As much beauty, sophistication, history and culture as there was to be had—everything she saw, everything she did, reminded her of another place.

She was forever referring to the Tube as the El, the Thames as the Lake, and searching the skyline for architecture with its foundation at the far side of The Pond. Professionally speaking, the city had become another stepping stone. The new project another rung on the ladder to success. A place to regain her perspective, hone her skills and build her résumé. Personally, it had been the redemption she'd needed, but at too high a cost.

London was not a place she could stay. Everything she'd given up to get there loomed in the shadows of her achievements, like ghosts she couldn't escape. Couldn't touch.

Jake.

She was ready to move on. Ready for the next stop.

Pushing through the turnstile door to her building, she shouldered her laptop and headed through the small lobby to the lift that would take her to her fourth-floor flat.

She slumped against the side of the tiny car, blindly watching the floors pass through the iron grate as she let herself drift back to the easy curve of Jake's lips and the low rumble of the laughter he gave so freely. Maybe she should call him again.

Her hand was fishing through her pocket before she'd even processed the thought, but as soon as her fingers closed around the phone she recognized her folly.

She didn't know if he was angry or if he'd already moved on. If he missed their friendship or thought about her at all. The only thing she knew for certain was how empty she felt.

Her eyes closed against the familiar stab of pain that accompanied the tormenting visions of a life she'd sacrificed on the altar of her pride. Visions of waking in Jake's bed every morning. Pouring him a drink as they listened to jazz by the fire at night. Laughing in his arms.

Loving in his arms.

She'd been so hung up on the words she'd lost sight of what had been right in front of her. The caring.

People talked of commitment all the time, only to have the relationship turn to dust. She'd been wearing Erik's ring when he'd betrayed her. Jake had been married when he'd been betrayed. The *words* hadn't mattered.

But what she felt when she was with him…the way he looked at her…some things—some people—were worth the risk. She just hadn't been willing to take it. To wait. To see how it played out. And now….

She missed him with an intensity time and distance had yet to ease.

Hell. Her eyes were wet again, and her soul felt as if it was trying to tear free from her body. The lift crept toward her floor, groaning, it seemed, under the strain of her heartbreak.

Her hand was still wrapped around the phone. She pulled it out, and her thumb brushed across the flat screen, bringing up the first of too many ways to contact Jake Tyler.

Blinking back her tears, she swiped at the emotional leakage with her wrist and shook her head. For a woman so set on moving forward, she wasn't exactly letting go of the past. The car slowed and Cali adjusted her shoulder bag as she reached for the grate—only to have it opened from the other side.

Her heart stopped.

"Hey, babe. Hope I didn't keep you waiting too long." The low baritone voice came like a midnight fantasy, riding words from what seemed a lifetime ago. It shocked her senses, slipping under her skin, warming through her body and confusing her mind like too much sweet wine.

Jake. He couldn't be real.

Her bags dropped to the floor with a loud thump and her breath rushed out in a whoosh, leaving scant air for words. "I'm hallucinating," she wheezed, certain this had something to do with a serious lack of sleep and an excess of longing.

The corner of Jake's mouth pulled up to the side as he shouldered into the small car.

He couldn't be real. Couldn't—

His arm, solid and strong, snaked around her waist, pulling her into the muscled planes of his body in a mesh of hard against soft, so perfectly right imagination couldn't have created it.

"Oh, my God, Jake."

His mouth was a breath above hers, painfully far and teasingly close all at once. "Sorry about the 'babe' business, but it does have that possessive quality I'm going for." His deep blue gaze held hers, searching, pleading. "Cali."

The arms that had gone limp at her sides were jolted into use by her name on his lips. They shot up and grasped the loose lapels of his open trench coat, dragging him down to her open, desperate mouth.

Jake. Here. An ocean away from where he was supposed to be. She should ask him a question—say something—but all that mattered were his fingers threading into the hair at the nape of her neck. Tilting her head back, opening her wider to him as he sank deeper into the kiss. Filling her with his tongue, his heat. She melted against his body, her knees went liquid, and her belly turned in on itself.

His arms tightened around her waist and back as he straightened to his full height, lifting her from her feet in the process. His lips never left hers, never stopped moving across her mouth in that sensual glide, his tongue sliding over and around hers.

Heaven help her, she was drowning in the taste of him. The scent. The touch. He shot through her system, a mainline to pleasure, hitting her like a drug she couldn't give up.

Her mouth moved frantically against his, breaking away only to kiss a new spot on his lips, around his jaw, his neck, ears, nose and eyes.

Again and again she kissed every spot she could find, tasting her own salty relief on his skin. She framed the chiseled features of his beautiful face with trembling hands, stroked a thumb over the slight stubble of his jaw. Met the endless blue of his stare.

"Tears?" he rasped in his husky tone, his gaze brushing her cheeks.

"Happy tears," she managed. After weeks of agony, one minute in his arms had replaced it all with elation. How could she have thought she could live without him?

"Happy is definitely good," he answered quietly, then closed his eyes and touched his brow to hers. "I'd almost forgotten what it felt like, but it's coming back to me fast."

Cocooned in the security of his arms, she felt a breath she'd been holding forever slip free, pulling the vise around her heart loose with it. "I've missed you so much… I thought—" She shook her head, looked into his face, needing to see him, to tell him everything.

Their surroundings caught her attention then—the small lift, her toes dangling inches above the floor. A quiet laugh escaped as a warm flush spread across her cheeks. "We should…my apartment…."

"Yeah." The corner of Jake's mouth kicked up in what appeared to be a grin. Then it was lost as his mouth crushed hers again, possessive and hot, blanking her mind of anything beyond the perfection of his taste. Too fast, it was over. She was on her feet, blinking wildly to bring reality back into focus.

Jake stood with her bags slung over one broad shoulder, offering his hand. "Ready?"

She nodded and slipped her palm into his, felt the warmth of his hold radiate up her arm, spread, tingling, through a body that had been numb to anything but pain since the day she'd torn it apart from the man it recognized as her other half.

"Definitely ready," she answered, and led him down the narrow hall to her door.

Inside the two-room flat, Jake set down her bags. Cali watched as he navigated around the clustered furniture to the window. Drawing the shade to find little more than a facing brick wall, he turned back, a smile tugging at his lips. It was bliss to see him filling the space she'd occupied for the last month, the space where she'd fantasized about him—hungered for him, never dreamed he would actually be.

"Nice place Amanda's got you in."

She laughed, seeing the tiny flat through his eyes. "Yeah, I don't think she had any connections setting this one up."

He leaned a shoulder against the window frame, crossing his arms over his chest, his chiseled features relaxed, warm, as he surveyed her. "You been doing well?"

She waved a dismissive hand, suddenly unsure of her own response. "There are any number of ways to answer, depending on how I'm looking at it."

Jake arched a brow at her. "I'm in London for three days, so I've got time to hear all of them."

Three days. Only three. "Work's been very good. We're ahead of schedule."

He chuckled, jutting his chin at her. "Of course you are."

Cali shrugged, feeling amused until she met his gaze. The smile on her lips crumbled and she began to shake.

Within two strides Jake had his arms around her. He pulled her into his lap on the couch. "Ah, sweetheart, don't cry."

"I've missed you," she whispered brokenly, a harsh sob catching in her throat. "So much. Every minute. I knew what I was doing when I left. I knew the choice I was making. But…the way it hurts…. I was so stupid. I thought I'd never get a chance to be with you again." She choked over the ragged words, blinking in a battle against tears that had clearly already won the war. "I can't believe you're here."

"I couldn't stay away," he soothed, stroking a hand down the soft tumble of her hair, the delicate bones in her back. "I tried. I really did. But life without you was empty." Horrible. Unbearable. He'd been so angry when she'd left. He'd tried to close himself off from his feelings, tried to believe being apart was for the best, but he'd been a fool.

There had been no peace. No relief. Nothing but the aching void growing steadily within him from the moment he'd left her at the airport. Before that. From the moment he'd realized he wouldn't be able to change her mind.

The hours had passed, and then the days. The weeks after that. He'd expected it would only be a matter of time until he was back on track, relieved by the return to the life of his design. He'd told himself Cali had been complicated. Messy. Everything he hadn't wanted but had somehow gotten bound up in. Only it wasn't true.

He'd gone out. With colleagues for drinks. With friends for dinner.

To the Jazz House for something—something he didn't find.

The music had poured over him, only he'd been numb to the melodies, refusing to feel the heartache and hope infused in every long-drawn note. A woman had slid onto the barstool beside him and struck up a light conversation, looking for a little company. Sensual invitation had shone in her eyes as she'd mentioned she'd only be in town for the night. At one time she would have been a perfect diversion. Temporary. Sexy. Easy.

But no longer.

He'd left the club with his heart slamming against his chest, his soul an open wound. It wasn't like it had been after Pam. Not even close. And it wasn't getting better. Still he'd refused to see the truth. He'd gone home and gotten on the treadmill, determined to beat himself out of his ever-deepening funk by pounding through the miles until his consciousness had been reduced to the draw and push of his breath, the repetitive thud of his feet. Only no matter how hard or far he'd pushed, she'd been there with him. Hovering at the edge of his mind.

Cali laughing as she discovered a jello mold while riffling through his cabinets.

Cali stretching that languorous stretch of hers some Sunday morning.

Asking him what he wanted for dinner. Smiling as she caught sight of him waiting outside her office to pick her up. Sighing as she fell asleep in his arms.

They were regular things. Nothing particularly special or different about them. Nothing unique. Except somehow they were. Somehow, with her, everything was different. Deeper. Stronger. More vibrant and intense. More than it had ever been with Pam... Because with Cali it was real. Right.

More than he'd ever imagined he wanted. So much more than he could live without.

Sweat streaming off him, he'd slapped the stop button, doubled forward, struck by the singular truth of the situation. The agony of the realization that he'd let her go before understanding it himself.

Cali. Cali. Cali….

Even now, with her tucked in his arms, he could barely breathe for thinking of how close he'd come to losing everything.

He rested his temple at hers, closing his eyes and basking in the heat of her body against him. "I want to be with you. I can give you what you're looking for, Cali. I was too scared— too blind to see that I already had. You have my heart. You have my future. I'll give you forever any way you want it. *I love you.* Like I didn't even know it could be, I love you."

She met his gaze, and the emotion in her glistening emerald eyes shattered him.

"I love you, too," she whispered. "From the first night, and a little more every day. I'm…lost without you."

She loved him. His heart swelled, relief washing over him in a wave.

He shook his head, dropping a slow, lazy kiss against her lips before pulling back to meet her eyes again. "I can't believe I'm saying this, but I'm glad you came—"

He broke off, stroked her face, met her eyes.

"I get how important this job is to you, that you had something you needed to prove to yourself. And I'm glad you did it. I needed time…to figure out myself."

"Oh, Jake…." Her voice was cracking. But he wanted her to understand, not to hurt.

"But it doesn't have to be one or the other, sweetheart. I can support you in your dreams and still be there with you, because more than anything I need you. We'll make this work, Cali. Whatever it takes. Just believe in me."

"I do." She smiled, brushing her fingers through his hair,

touching the shell of his ear, tracing the tendon of his neck. "I still can't believe you're here."

He chuckled. "Yeah, it took me weeks to rearrange my surgery schedule and bribe my old med school roommate into letting me pick up his talk at the cardiac conference here tomorrow."

Cali slipped her arms around his neck. "You didn't…." She half sighed as he nibbled his way across her collarbone.

"Mmm, but I did," he murmured, his fingers drifting along the buttons of her shirt. "I've rearranged my patient appointments and my surgery schedule to be in London for six of the next eight weekends—with a few four-day stretches at that."

She stilled in his arms and met his gaze. "Jake, we're ahead of schedule. I'm leaving London in four weeks."

Ahead of schedule. Just like Chicago. He should have figured.

"Doesn't matter. I'll visit wherever you are." His hands slipped between the open lapels of her shirt, smoothing over the creamy skin it had been too long since he'd touched. "Where are you headed next?"

When she didn't answer, Jake dragged his attention from the lacy mounds to her eyes. She was staring back at him with too much focus for a woman whose shirt was open to her belly button.

The very tip of her tongue touched the full swell of that lush bottom lip of hers, lingering over a weighted pause that had his body less interested in where she was moving for work and more interested in moving her into the bedroom.

"Chicago. I've taken a permanent position as Midwest Regional Manager."

He froze, struck dumb and immobilized by her response.

"I've met my promise to myself. Now all I want is to be

happy, and in my whole life I've never been as happy as I was there."

Her palms flattened against his chest, her gaze dropping in blatant appreciation of what she found there. His little Cali, who had a sweet tooth for man-candy and didn't get kissed often enough. He leaned forward, caught her mouth with his, swept a teasing stroke of his tongue between her lips.

Her fingers balled in the fabric of his shirt as her velvety sigh warmed his mouth. "If you want," she whispered, "we can be happy there together."

"Marry me." The words were out before he'd even thought to say them. But he had no desire to take them back. "More than anything, I want you to marry me."

This time Cali froze.

This wasn't the way he'd planned, but it wasn't impulse or desperation either. It was right. "I'll love you forever. I'll make you happy, sweetheart. I swear I can."

Her lips trembled and a single tear slipped from the corner of her eye. Her hands tightened in his shirt as though she were trying to contain him—as if he weren't hers already. He pulled her against his chest, murmuring into the delicate curve of her neck, "Marry me."

She pulled back to meet his stare, smile spreading, green eyes shining. "Yes," she answered, her breath catching on something between a laugh and sigh. "Yes!" she said again, the sound of her voice so rich and sweet. Certain. "I'll marry you."

"Thank God," he answered, with utter sincerity.

The laugh that had first snared his heart bubbled free, and then Cali was covering him with her body and her mouth, showering him in a flurry of kisses, tugging at his clothes, groaning at the sight of his bare chest and driving him wild as only she could.

He'd never have enough of her.

His hands were at her shoulders, his heart slamming against his ribs as he turned and pinned her to the cushions beneath him. His shirt hung open, half off his shoulders. He had to stop before they got any further.

"Wait right here." Grinning, he tried to escape from the couch.

Her leg hooked around his hip, pulling him back to her, and a little pout formed on her mouth. "We've waited long enough."

Braced on one arm above her, Jake let his head drop forward as he chuckled. "It'll be worth it; just give me one second."

Cali peered up at him through her lashes, an impish glint in her eyes. "I'll give you my whole life…." She bit into that lush bottom lip of hers, pulled it slowly from the clasp of her teeth—damn, that worked for him—before she finished. "If you give me the next few minutes of yours."

Swallowing hard, Jake glanced at where his coat lay, draped over the bags he'd carried in for her, then back to the woman running her hands over his stomach. "God, I love you."

Her fingers caught in the waist of his pants and she tugged him down on top of her.

"I love you, too," she whispered, holding him with her lustrous green-eyed gaze. The corner of her mouth curved as her knee skimmed up his side. "And I'm not letting you go."

As a man committed to making his wife-to-be happy, Jake closed his lips over hers, then sank into a kiss that tasted like heaven and promised forever. The three-karat diamond ring parked in the interior pocket of his overcoat would have to wait…just a few minutes more.